A DEADLY SECRET

Imperiled Young Widows, Book 3

Melanie Dickerson

GraceFaith Press

ASIN: B09T4Y5SB7

ISBN: 9798421511571

Cover design by: Erin Dameron-Hill
Library of Congress Control Number: 2018675309
Printed in the United States of America

To Aaron
I have found the one
my soul loves

CONTENTS

A DEADLY SECRET

CHAPTER ONE

Early Summer, 1811, the Isle of Wight

The wind blew hard from the sea, whipping her three-year-old's wispy blond hair over her face.

Lillian Courtney glanced over her shoulder, little Bella's hand in hers, as they walked from the small stable and carriage house to the cottage on the hill.

Her grandfather's cottage looked older than she remembered, with one of the shutters on the upper floor hanging askew. Five years had passed since she'd been there, but with its quaint thatched roof and flowering vines climbing the rock wall, it was still a beautiful sight.

She did not even like thinking her husband's Christian name. It was easier to call him "Bella's father" or "my husband" or "Mr. Courtney." Sometimes, late at night when Bella was asleep, Lillian would imagine that she'd never married the wealthy gentleman who'd recently inherited the vast Stokemont Abbey estate in Gloucestershire, England. She imagined refusing Mr. Courtney's proposal of marriage and marrying someone else. She never imagined who that someone else might be, but in her imaginings, little Bella was always their child.

She never told anyone of these daydreams, as she was probably committing some sin by having them. At least her pretend husband was not a real person, was no one that she'd ever met, and had no distinct features. But he was kind and loving, always affectionate, and adoring of both her and their child.

Tomorrow she would go into the village and see about hiring a servant for her stay, but for tonight, she and her daughter were alone. After a lifetime of being cared for by servants, it was a strange feeling, and yet not an altogether unwelcome one.

Lillian unlocked the door with her key, remembering how her family had grumbled upon hearing that her grandfather had left Lillian this house, settling it irrevocably on her, so that whomever she married could not take possession of it. Later, when she married Mr. Courtney, she quickly sensed that her new husband was also not pleased about the cottage her grandfather had gifted her.

"The Isle of Wight? That is not a fashionable place, is it?" Her husband frowned, a sour look on his face.

"It's in an old fishing village where my grandfather's family once lived."

"Perhaps you shouldn't mention the place to any of our acquaintances." Her husband had sniffed and glanced around the room, never looking at Lillian at all.

Lillian was careful not to speak of it, as the subject was obviously distasteful to him.

She was intuitive enough to figure out, in the early days of their marriage, what her husband liked and disliked, and she learned to avoid speaking of anything that might set off his volatile temper. Among the subjects she avoided were her family members, any friends he disapproved of, which she soon learned was all of her friends, and anything that wasn't particularly flattering to him.

It was nearly dark when they arrived, so Lillian set about starting a fire in the fireplace. The task proved more difficult than she had imagined, as she'd watched fires being built all her life. Why should it be so hard?

Finally, after using the old matches she found, along with some bits of paper and cloth that seemed purposely left next to the fireplace, she managed to get a tiny fire going. She used the small fire to light the larger pieces of wood. Then she lit some candles and she and Bella sat on the floor with the supplies Lillian had brought.

"We shall have a fine picnic. We have cheese and butter and bread, see? And I brought your favorite, apple tart."

Bella smiled when she saw the tart and ate it first.

While Bella ate, she held her doll under her arm. Seeing the child holding onto her doll brought back the memory of two weeks ago, when Mrs. Courtney, her husband's mother, had come to fetch them for a holiday to Brighton.

"Isabella, put down the doll and go to your grandmother," her husband ordered.

Bella's mouth clamped shut and she clutched the ragged doll tighter to her chest.

"We're going on a trip," Mrs. Courtney said, "and

you won't need that ratty old thing." She made a grimace, as though the doll was the most disgusting thing imaginable. "Come. Your Grandmamma shall buy you a new doll. You would like a new doll, would you not?"

Bella shook her head and held the doll against her cheek, putting her thumb in her mouth.

"Isabella, take your thumb out of your mouth." Lillian's husband's voice was stern, his expression hard.

"Yes, take your thumb out of your mouth, dear." Mrs. Courtney again looked disgusted. "Nasty habit. Shameful and nasty. That's what dirty beggars' children do, and you are a Courtney, a gentleman's daughter, not a dirty beggar's child."

Lillian's heart was pounding, her stomach sick, at the tears welling up in her child's eyes. She wanted nothing more than to take her child in her arms and run from the room. But she was too afraid of what her mother-in-law and husband would do. No doubt it would have repercussions for Bella and only make things worse. So Lillian tried to be diplomatic.

"I don't think this will gain the desired result," Lillian said, using a light tone to diminish the tension in the air. Her husband's jawline hardened, his brows lowered, and his eyes narrowed.

She took a step toward her daughter, who immediately raised her hand, asking to be picked up, with her other hand still clutching the doll close. When she bent to pick up Bella, out of the corner of her eye, she saw her husband step toward her.

Suddenly something hit her in the back and she pitched forward. As she did, she clasped Bella with one arm while throwing her other hand on the floor, desperate to catch herself before she should fall on Bella.

Lillian's knees hit the floor, hard. She held on to Bella, protecting her from hitting the floor.

Bella's free hand was wrapped around Lillian's neck, her other still clutching her doll.

Lillian realized her husband had shoved her from behind. She could still feel where his hands had hit her.

Shame washed over her in a wave of heat that made her cheeks burn. Her knees were hurting, but the pain was nothing to the fury that pulsed through her. How dare he endanger Bella? How dare he strike her at all, but especially when she was holding their daughter?

With as much dignity as she could muster, Lillian stood to her feet, enfolding Bella protectively with both arms.

"Well," Mrs. Courtney was saying emphatically, "this is why we keep a nurse. Where is the child's nurse? Every child needs a proper nurse."

How did her husband dare? And Mrs. Courtney . . . how could she just ignore what he had done, pretending the fact that the nurse wasn't present had caused this.

Bella's eyes were wide, her gaze trained on her mother, as if waiting for an explanation, still holding on to her neck. *God, I pray Bella doesn't understand what just happened.*

Her husband stood with his arms folded across his chest while Mrs. Courtney kept talking, ordering and instructing, still ignoring what had actually happened.

"The child's nurse will take her in her lap in the carriage on the journey and will be able to amuse the child." Turning all her attention on Bella, she said in a high-pitched voice, "We shall sing songs and play games all the way to Brighton."

With all her heart and strength, Lillian wanted to

refuse to go to Brighton. But the servants were loading their trunks in the carriage at that moment. And her mother-in-law would insist on taking the child with them, but Lillian was not letting Bella go anywhere without her.

"Look at George," Mrs. Courtney instructed Bella. "He's being such a good boy, and everyone loves George. Isabella, isn't George a good boy? You should be like George. He doesn't make a fuss." Mrs. Courtney's voice was strident, no longer placating.

George was five years old, the child of Lillian's husband's younger sister, and he spent so much time with his grandmother, Lillian wondered if he ever saw his own parents. From a few comments Mrs. Courtney had made, Lillian suspected she'd prefer to take charge of Bella in just the same way.

"My dear, you look pale," Mrs. Courtney said, regarding Lillian with a pointed stare. "If you prefer to stay here, we can take Isabella with us. She will have a merry time with George, and you can rest."

Her husband still said not a word.

"No, I am very well. I believe all is ready."

They departed soon after, and the trip was as miserable as Lillian had feared, but she never let Bella out of her sight, refusing to let her mother-in-law take the child anywhere without her. Though Mrs. Courtney did try, several times.

"This is an outing just for the children and me," she would say, but Lillian would always find an excuse to either go with them or to keep Bella with her in their hired rooms.

Lillian had seen enough of the strange way her mother-in-law would alternately criticize unjustly, then praise undeservedly, those she seemed to love most. She did it with her son as well as her grandson, mostly when she thought Lillian wasn't paying attention. It seemed to be her odd way of controlling them.

Lillian had once heard Mrs. Courtney say, speaking to Lillian's husband, "Don't sing in church. Your voice is terrible, and you make everyone around you miserable. You can't carry a tune in a bucket, just like your father." Half an hour later, she was saying, "Everyone loves you! In school you were the most popular boy, and you are still admired. There is no one more perfect or more well-liked than you."

Of course, it was rubbish. Lillian's husband wasn't particularly well-liked at all, and she herself, as his wife, had liked him less and less as he unleashed his unpredictable and angry temperament on her.

"It isn't healthy to always keep the child with you," Mrs. Courtney scolded Lillian. "You need time away, and she needs time away from her mother. That is what the nurse is for."

Lillian did not disagree, but she had explained in detail to both her mother-in-law and to her husband why she found it difficult to leave Bella completely in the care of a nurse.

When Lillian and her brother Christopher were young, their nurse treated them very ill, doling out severe punishments for imagined infractions, beating them and locking them in dark closets. Christopher had suffered the most, and he never seemed to fully recover, possessing a deep-seated anger that emerged when she least expected it.

Indeed, her husband's anger sometimes reminded her of her brother's.

But her mother-in-law and husband never acknowledged her explanation of her past and why she did not wish to leave her own child's care completely to someone else, as was common.

When they finally arrived back home to Stokemont Abbey after their trip to Brighton, Lillian could see from her husband's demeanor that he was about to lash out at her.

He came to her bedroom after she'd prepared for bed. She was sitting at her dressing table, brushing her hair. He started pacing up and down the floor, then crossed his arms and stood glaring at her.

Lillian gripped the hairbrush in her hand. *God,* she prayed, *give me the courage to hit him if he tries to harm me.* The memory of him striking her in the back and knocking her to the floor was still fresh.

Her husband stopped pacing and stared at her, his arms folded over his chest.

"Why do you disrespect me the way you do? And in front of my mother?"

"I don't disrespect you." Her breath was becoming shallow, and she gripped the hairbrush tighter.

"You spoil the child, letting her have that doll, and when my own mother tries to talk her into putting it down . . ."

His voice grew louder and more strident with every word, while Lillian's heart thumped harder in her chest.

"I told you to let the nurse take care of the child and stop pretending she needs you. I know your father was in trade before he sold his business, but I thought you wished to be a respectable lady in good social standing. The women in our social circles do not take so much time with their children." His face was beginning to turn red, as he was now shouting at her and pointing his finger in her face. "I married you because I thought you were docile, always smiling and laughing at all the parties where I saw you, and I thought you would be happy to be my wife. But you are never happy. You can't be happy. You refuse to be happy! And you have defied me at every turn. You are a rebellious woman."

The expression on his face sent a chill into her heart. Indeed, his sneering lips and his dark eyes seemed to speak nothing but loathing.

"You have nothing to say for yourself, do you? You probably want me to strike you so that you can tell all your friends that I beat you." His voice was lower now, calmer. "I am finished with you. Do as you wish."

With those words, he stalked from the room.

She did not see him for five days, neither knowing nor much caring where he was. The house was much more peaceful without him.

When he returned, however, he had been drinking, and he continued to drink for several more hours. The day ended with him coming into her room at bedtime, as before, and shouting angrily at her.

"Please go to bed," she told him in as stern a tone as she could muster. "You need to sleep." With that, she turned away from him.

He hit her in the back before she could brace herself —once, twice—and then she ran from the room.

She hid herself in an empty bedroom until she heard him go to his own room and slam the door.

She slept that night in the nursery, curled up next to Bella in her small bed. While her daughter slept, Lillian wept, her tears flowing silently into the pillow.

I was always smiling and laughing before I married

you. She imagined speaking the words aloud to her husband. She had thought herself strong, that she would never allow her husband to treat her badly. Her grandfather once told her never to stay with a man who would hit her, that nothing justified a husband's laying hands in anger on his wife, who was his precious gift from God. And she promised him—and herself—that she would never stand for such a thing. Now it was time for her to fulfill that promise.

The next morning she rose and, finding her husband gone, packed a trunk of things for herself and Bella, and left. She did not leave a note and told no one where she was going.

Now, as Lillian laid Bella's sleeping form in the bed, she remembered how much she had enjoyed being here in this cottage when her grandfather was alive, and sleeping in this very bed as a child.

"We're safe here," she whispered.

How beautiful her Isabella was, with her baby face and plump cheeks, her eyes closed, and her body in a posture of complete trust and repose. *God, help me keep her safe from harm. I don't want her to have horrific memories of her childhood.*

These days, most of her prayers were much shorter than this, sometimes just, "God, help me." Her rote prayers that she'd memorized from infancy were often cut to snippets, so scattered and harassed were her thoughts.

To keep them both from being awakened by the cold, Lillian fetched the warming pan, slipping it between the blankets and the sheet.

Surely Bella's father wouldn't think to look for them here. In fact, he might accuse her of abandonment and pursue a divorce. *Please, God, let him divorce me.*

Perhaps she shouldn't pray for that, as it would doubtlessly cause so many problems, if it were even possible, but she could see no other way out. She was trapped in a sort of bondage to a man who would strike her—and not even to her face, or always in their private rooms, but in the back and in the presence of other people.

She pushed away those heavy, overwhelming thoughts and began listing the practical ways she had to support herself.

Aside from this cottage that her grandfather had left her, her father had settled a sum of money on her that should be just enough to provide for her and Bella. They could live here on the Isle of Wight quite comfortably, though it was an unfashionable place. What did she care about fashion? She was bent on survival.

Perhaps she was hoping beyond what was reasonable by thinking she and Bella could live on their own. Her husband might hate her and never care to see her or his child again, but his mother would never let her take Bella away from his family. In fact, Mrs. Courtney might try to take Bella from her. And this was how they could force her to go back to her husband, for she could not lose Bella. She could not turn her over to that smothering woman, who criticized with sharp, unjust cruelty one minute, and praised the same person just as unreasonably the next. In this way, Lillian believed, the woman had turned her son into a man who could never accept that he ever did anything wrong, whose emotions were out of control, and who never took responsibility.

But perhaps running away had been a mistake. After all, now Lillian would be looking over her shoulder every day, wondering when her husband would come after her. And many people would see her actions as wrong. Perhaps she would never have friends again, people who would care about her or offer her aid.

She lay awake for a long time with these terrifying thoughts whirling around and around in her mind. But if she didn't think about them, she wouldn't be prepared. And she had to prepare for the inevitable battle, for she would not stay with a husband who abused her, and she would rather die than let Mrs. Courtney take her child. Bella was everything, now that Mother and Father had passed away and Christopher was married to Gretchen.

But she wouldn't think about Christopher's wife. Not now. That woman was far enough away in northern Hampshire, and far away was where she preferred to keep her. Besides, Gretchen could neither want nor need anything from Lillian.

Unfortunately, she could not say the same for Mrs. Courtney.

~ ~ ~

On their third day in the little fishing village on the Isle of Wight, Lillian and Bella were walking home after buying food.

She still had not inquired about hiring a servant. Making inquiries would require her to reveal more about herself than she cared to share, such as the fact that she was married but living away from her husband. And telling anyone her name was certainly too much information.

Lillian slowed her steps to match Bella's tiny stride as they walked up the narrow lane to the thatched-roof, two-story cottage.

A movement caused her to glance to her right, across the moorland heather. Walking toward them was a man, still a hundred feet away. And she was reasonably sure he was her husband.

She scooped her daughter up in her arms, awkwardly bundling her with the bag of food she had bought.

"We're almost there," she said cheerfully. She quickened her pace, hoping Bella would not see her father.

Quickly unlocking the door, Lillian hurried inside just as she heard her husband's voice call her name.

She put her bag on the floor and shut the door. Then she locked it and moved the crossbar into place.

"What's wrong, Mamma?" Bella put her tiny hand on Lillian's cheek.

"Nothing, my sweeting. All is well." She hurried them to the bedroom where they'd slept the night before, just as a knock came at the front door.

"It's all right. We will stay where we are. All is well," she kept reassuring Bella, who looked more curious than afraid.

"Are we playing hide-and-seek?" Bella asked.

"Yes, of a sort."

Lillian tried to think if she'd left any windows open. She hurried to the back of the cottage, still holding Bella in her arms, and slammed the window shut that she had left open to let in the warm summer air. She checked to make sure the back door's crossbar was in place, then hurried back to the bedroom.

Then the pounding and shouting started, as she could hear her husband's angry voice.

Instead of listening to what he was saying, she sat with Bella on the bed and sang her favorite songs and nursery rhymes. But her own voice was starting to sound high-pitched and nervous. And Bella was growing fidgety.

When she heard her husband pounding on the back door, her heart pounded just as hard. Would he break a window to get in? She couldn't keep him out if he was determined enough.

Finally, the pounding stopped.

But he'd be back.

~ ~ ~

It was morning. Lillian went to the window and peeked out through a crack in the shutters. The sun was just up, no more than an hour ago.

She took a deep breath, feeling calmer than she had since her husband had pounded on the door the day before. Thankfully, she'd heard nothing from him since then.

Someone knocked on the front door. Lillian's heart lurched.

"Mrs. Courtney?" a voice called, barely audible. It was a man's voice, but it did not sound like her husband's.

Lillian left Bella asleep on the bed, tiptoed to the front of the house, and peeked out the window.

A group of four men were standing at the door. She quickly examined each face. None looked like her husband, although one of them caught her looking out the window.

"Mrs. Courtney," he called, "we need to speak with you."

"Can you wait a moment until I'm dressed?" she called back.

"Yes, madam." The man and his companions looked patient enough.

Lillian hurried back to the room and dressed herself, hindered by the shaking of her hands. Finally, she went back to the front of the house, again looking to make sure her husband was not with them, then opened the door.

"Pardon us, Mrs. Courtney, for this intrusion." The man who'd spoken to her through the door introduced himself as the constable and the man beside him as the coroner. "We are most abominably sorry to tell you that we found your husband's body early this morning, just before sunrise. It appears he fell from the cliff to the beach below, not half a mile from here."

Lillian stared at the man as her thoughts exploded like a gun going off. "My husband?"

"Is your husband tall, with blond hair and a small scar just here, on his chin?"

"Yes."

"I am very sorry, madam. Your husband has died. It was a very long fall, you see, and—"

"Mamma?"

Lillian turned and lifted her precious little girl into her arms as both relief and horror washed over her. *At least we are safe now.*

So why was she crying?

CHAPTER TWO

Lillian did not go back to Gloucestershire for her husband's funeral. Only men attended funerals anyway, as women were discouraged from attending—partially for practical reasons of safety, as funeral processions and funerals occurred late at night, and partially because it was simply the custom among the wealthy and fashionable for the women to stay home.

Aside from that, Lillian was not ready to leave the safe haven she had found on the Isle of Wight in her grandfather's old cottage.

Several days after her husband's funeral would have taken place, a knock came at the door. She answered it to find a courier with a letter.

After paying and dismissing him, and while still standing in the doorway, she opened the letter. It was from her mother-in-law. It had taken her nearly a fortnight after her son's death to write.

Lillian knew she must read it, but she wished she didn't have to.

Lifting her head, she caught sight of a man staring

at her from the hill fifty feet away. What did the man mean, staring at her? A shiver passed over her shoulders as she stared back at him. Then he turned and walked in the opposite direction.

She tried to make note of him, of his nondescript clothing, which was that of a poor man, of his size and the tilt of his head and shoulders, the color of his hair. But he was soon too far away for her to see anything specific.

Lillian went inside and closed the door, dismissing the strange man from her thoughts.

Thankfully, Mrs. Courtney had not come for her son's body. She had sent her solicitor to collect her son's body and take it back to Gloucestershire and Stokemont Abbey.

The coroner had finished investigating, ruling it an accidental death brought on by his intoxicated state after drinking most of the night at the local public house.

"Being unfamiliar with the area, he must have stepped off the edge, as dark as it was, before he realized it," the coroner had stated.

Through her husband's death, God had saved Lillian from a very difficult life, but just thinking such a thought caused warring feelings of relief and guilt. A man was dead, the man she had once loved, had pledged her loyalty to, and with whom she shared a child. He was dead and had died so suddenly, he could not ask for forgiveness for his sins.

But perhaps he had not died immediately. Perhaps he'd had time to repent of the things he'd done wrong. She would never know for certain, but she could pray that it was so.

After she had settled Bella on the floor with her tiny tea set and she was happily feeding her doll her pretend tea, Lillian sat down to read her letter. Between its many blotches of ink, it was as though the writer had written with haste and strong emotion.

My Dear Daughter Lillian,

Allow me to express how shocked I was that you did not return home with your husband when Foster brought his body for burial in our own parish churchyard. My grief could have been greatly assuaged by dear little Isabella's comforting presence. But I suppose you did not think of that. Or perhaps you did.

My grief has been great indeed, nearly matched by my confusion over you taking our Isabella so far away, without telling me or your husband beforehand. And now this has all brought about my son's death. Your husband went to find you, to fetch you back, and now he is dead. I blame you.

How is this possible? Such things have never happened, not in our family, not in Gloucestershire, either. You have brought this about.

I sincerely hope you will do the right thing and bring back my dear son's child to me. I cannot go on without her. She is the dearest person in the world to me now. You must return her to her rightful family. Do not defy me in this, Lillian, or you will regret it.

Your Mother-in-Law,
Mrs. Edward Henshawe Courtney

Lillian's hand shook when she read the threat in the last line.

Mrs. Courtney blamed Lillian for her son's death, and she would not rest until she had Bella nearby, where she could see her every day and even take her to live with her, as she had Bella's cousin George. She wanted control over Bella.

Certainly, now that Lillian's husband was dead, and since she would inherit nothing from her husband, her mother-in-law had the wealth and power to take Bella from her.

She had little choice but to return to Gloucestershire. But she would fight for her daughter and would never give her up.

Her hands were still shaking as she found her lap desk and sat down. As she wrote, a tear slid down her cheek. She wiped it quickly to keep it from staining the paper.

Tomorrow she would pack up their things and make the journey back to Stokemont Abbey. But if Mrs. Courtney thought Lillian would be turning her daughter over to her to do with whatever she pleased, she was greatly mistaken. She would not let that woman take Bella from her. She would fight her through Chancery Court if necessary, and if all else failed, she'd take her daughter and go somewhere that woman would not find them.

Lillian was no sheep to be ordered and led wheresoever her mother-in-law wished.

Yes, she would go back to Gloucestershire, and she would let Mrs. Courtney see her granddaughter, but she would not be staying long at Stokemont Abbey. Her husband's brother was the new owner now, and Lillian would be only a guest, and certainly an unwelcome one.

She'd find some way to keep Bella out of Mrs. Courtney's grasp, no matter what she had to do or where she had to live.

~ ~ ~

Two days later, Lillian and Bella boarded the boat

that would take them across the Channel.

She noticed a man staring at her from the dock. Was it the same man she'd seen staring at her from the moorland hill above her grandfather's cottage? But she lost sight of him in the crowd of people. She didn't see him again, and soon the boat was on its way on what would be a quick journey from the island to the mainland.

Her heavy heart focused on the twelve-hour coach trip to Stokemont Abbey, the home she'd shared with her husband. She only hoped Bella would sleep most of the way. There wasn't much else for a three-year-old to do, sitting on her mother's lap for a whole day.

She occupied her time trying to think how best to placate Mrs. Courtney while keeping Bella safe. Perhaps she could rent a small cottage near enough to Stokemont Abbey that Mrs. Courtney would not be able to say Bella was too far away for visits, but far enough away to make it impossible to see her every day.

She had not factored in the expense of paying for lodgings. But somehow her living would have to be enough.

~ ~ ~

Lillian entered the drawing room with Bella's little arms wrapped around her neck.

"Oh, my Isabella!" Mrs. Courtney cried out, extending her arms toward Bella from across the room.

At first Bella seemed reluctant to get down, but after a few moments, she loosened her grip on Lillian's neck, allowed her mother to set her down on the floor, and went slowly toward Mrs. Courtney.

"Oh, my sweet Isabella." Mrs. Courtney clasped Bella to her bosom, picking her up and placing her in her lap. The woman was making whimpering noises, pretending to cry, but there were no tears in her eyes.

She held the child so long and so tightly, that Bella began to squirm, trying to push away from her grandmother, and when she did not let her go, Bella began to cry.

"Come, now, don't cry," Mrs. Courtney said in a hushed voice, finally drawing away and letting Bella breathe. Mrs. Courtney's own eyes were red-rimmed. "I shall buy you a pony. Do you want a pony? Are you hungry? Do you want something sweet? Cook has made some sweet cakes for you. Anything you want, I will get it for you. You just tell your grandmamma what you want."

Bella stared back at her, wide-eyed.

"Your old nurse is here, Susanna. You remember your nurse." Mrs. Courtney motioned with her hand and Bella's nurse came into the room.

Bella barely looked at Susanna. No doubt Bella was confused and overwhelmed by her grandmother's insistent attitude, overly emotional state, and offers to buy her anything she wanted.

"She is very tired from our journey," Lillian said. She would not be intimidated by the woman's cold, scornful look. "After a good night's sleep, I'm sure she will be well and—"

"You are tired, I think," Mrs. Courtney said, interrupting her. "Go to bed. We shall tend to the child for you and you can rest. Go on."

Mrs. Courtney turned to Bella, dandling her on her knee. "We shall let your mamma rest and we shall be merry and blithe. Yes, we shall."

Bella turned around and reached out for her mother with a whimper.

"Isabella, listen. We shall go to the kitchen and get some cake and candy and anything else you might fancy. Shall we? Come." Mrs. Courtney stood with Bella in her arms.

"Mamma," Bella cried, her eyes pleading.

Lillian went to her and took her from Mrs. Courtney, letting Bella press her cheek against hers. "I am sorry. She needs to go to bed now. We shall see you in the morning."

Lillian hurried from the room, fully aware of Mrs. Courtney's glare.

"She is too attached to you," Mrs. Courtney called out. "You will make the child nervous."

Lillian ignored the words as she talked softly to Bella, walking up the stairs and placing Bella in her old nursery bed.

She couldn't bear to go to her own room, the place where her husband had struck her in the back on her last night here. So, when Bella was asleep, Lillian lay down beside her, closed her eyes, and tried not to think.

~ ~ ~

Nash Golding heard his mother call to him from down the hall.

He quickly put down his pen and slapped a sheet of paper over the page he was writing, stuffed the finished pages in his desk, and stood up quickly. When he did, he knocked over the inkwell.

Scrambling to set it upright, he spilled a bit on his thumb and had to reach for a cloth, which he kept beside his desk for just such a purpose.

"I'm in here, Mother," he called, wiping his hand and surveying his desk to make sure she would see nothing suspicious.

"There you are." His mother smiled as she entered the room. "Writing more letters?"

"Grandfather asked me to take over his letter writing, you know."

"The shaking in his hands has gotten a bit worse. The physicians all say that we will just have to wait and see if it improves." Mother frowned.

"Yes, Mother. Did you need me?"

"Your aunt Genevieve and I thought to take a trip to London for a fortnight, and I know how much you enjoy the concerts and theatricals. Would you like to accompany us?"

No. His book was nearly finished. "I might just stay here and ... study. I have some books I've been wanting to read, and—"

Mother was frowning, a questioning look in her eyes. "Very well, although I don't know what you could be studying. You left the university, and you can read in London too, you know."

"I know, Mother, but you also know how much I enjoy the country, the quiet and solitude, in contrast with London's noise and smoke."

"Of course, but don't you ever long for the society of a young lady? You are of marrying age, you know." She raised her brows at him. "There aren't very many young ladies in Gloucestershire that you haven't already rejected."

"You make it sound as if I go around the countryside rejecting women who are in love with me." Which of course was ludicrous.

He'd never been very charming or confident when young ladies were around. In fact, he was certain to be just the opposite—awkward. And the lovelier the young lady, the worse it was. Truthfully, he rarely encountered a young lady who enjoyed conversing about the same subjects that he enjoyed, a lady who was genuine and did not try to impress him. And he'd yet to meet a lady who seemed to like him for himself and not his title and wealth.

"I just want you to be happy." Mother smiled sanguinely.

"I will be. That is, I am happy." Or at least, he would be . . . someday. "I shall marry, Mother. I am not quite old and decrepit just yet."

"You are neither old nor decrepit." She sighed and shook her head. "Someday you shall not be so quick to turn away the young ladies I find for you. Someday you shall value my opinion on who is well suited to you and your position in society."

His position in society, meaning the fact that he was the Earl of Barrentine and Viscount Holbrooke, a Member of the House of Lords, and responsible for the legacy of his family name and estates. But he knew his duty and he would fulfill it, to the best of his ability. Could he not also have something that he enjoyed, even if it would horrify and embarrass his mother and five sisters if they knew? Something that would keep him from being ordinary and dull, just another face and name that no one truly knew, understood, or remembered?

Nash had expressed his desire to be a writer to his father, before he died. His mother and sisters had discovered his first manuscript—a satirical novel based on the popular novels of the day, full of ghosts and haunted houses, and romantic entanglements between harsh, abusive older men and very young, innocent women.

There was so much he could satirize. And he did so

enjoy writing that first novel.

His mother, father, and sisters, however, were not amused.

"You cannot be thinking of letting anyone read this," his mother said.

"You are a peer of the realm, son," his father said, "and thus must conduct yourself with utmost dignity. Writing novels is no way for a future earl to conduct himself. What if one of my—one of *your*—political rivals were to discover a copy of your novel?"

How could he tell his father that he didn't wish to have political rivals? The idea of sitting in Parliament was dull in the extreme, but to take an active part, to be for and against other members and their ideologies, was detestable to him.

At the same time, he didn't want to be one of those titled lords who sat and slept through the sessions of Parliament, hardly caring about anything besides their next drink. He only wished he could care about his country and fellow man while not taking an active part in Parliament.

This had been his dilemma for many years. While his father was alive, he did not have to worry about it, but . . . Father had died two years before. And though Nash did his best to do his duty as a Member of the House of Lords and pay attention during sessions, he used his ample time outside of his Parliamentary duties to do what he enjoyed.

He'd made the mistake of telling his father, those five or so years ago, "I was hoping to publish my books under a pseudonym. No one would—"

"Publish? Publish a work of fiction? Such a thing is not done. No. You must put away this childish notion."

"Childish notion?" Nash had stared back at his father. "Even if I publish anonymously? No one will ever know."

"They will know. They always find out, and especially when one is a peer of the realm. Do you really think anything you do can be kept secret? Secrets do not exist in the peerage, not in this day of newspapers and their reporters, gossipmongers extraordinaire."

"Yes, Nash," his nearest sister, Mildred, said. "How can we ever get good husbands if our brother is a novelist? It's a vulgar occupation for a viscount and the heir of —"

"Hush up, Mildred. You have no say in this." Nash glared at his sister, and she scrunched up her face and crossed her eyes at him.

"Mildred, don't do that," his mother scolded. "And Nash, you should be kind to your sisters. If a prospective wife were to hear you speak to your sister that way—"

"I'm sorry, Mother." His spirits were too low to apologize to his sister, as his father—indeed, his whole family—had just destroyed his hopes for his future happiness. He had dreamed of publishing his writings. It was his dearest wish.

He tried to stop writing after that, telling himself that writing was not his future. He needed to be practical and dutiful as a son and brother and peer of the realm. But in ceasing to write, he sank into a deep depression.

After several months, he decided he would recommence writing, but he would do it secretly, and publish his works secretly. He would make sure no one ever knew his identity. He'd take on a new name and no one need know.

His family was wrong. He could keep it a secret.

CHAPTER THREE

Lillian hurried to the post office in the village of Gantt to see if she'd received any replies from her letters of inquiry.

She had written to every friend that her husband had not offended over the past five years, the ones who still spoke to her, and she found that there were only three. So, to the three of them she wrote to ask for the favor of their help in finding lodgings for herself and Bella, preferably in Gloucestershire or a neighboring county.

When she wrote, "Something inexpensive, in keeping with my reduced means," her cheeks burned a bit in embarrassment. Would her friends prove true? Or would they look on her as someone who was beneath them now?

No matter. The important thing was taking care of Bella and keeping them both safe from harm and the control of Mrs. Courtney.

She'd kept up a brisk pace in her walk from Stokemont Abbey to the village, as it was early, and though it was summer, this morning was cool. Her mother-in-law normally slept at least another hour or two, and she left Bella in the care of her nurse.

Now, as she turned to go inside the post office, a movement out of the corner of her eye made her turn her head in the direction of the Abbey, from which she had come.

A man was on the road, standing as if he had just stopped, as if he'd been following her. She was almost certain it was the man whom she had seen staring at her twice on the Isle of Wight—once outside her cottage and once at the dock.

Lillian quickly entered the post office, her heart beating hard and fast. Was she imagining that this man was following her, and that he was the same man she'd seen before?

She'd never been a particularly nervous person, but the events of the last few weeks had made her jump at every unexpected noise and awaken in the middle of the night, out of breath and with fearful thoughts whirling around in her head.

She must be rational. Her grandfather had not taught her to be fearful. If the man was still there when she left the post office, she would confront him and ask his name and what his business was with her.

The thought was a bit frightening, as the man did not appear to be a gentleman by his manner of dress, his walk, or his facial expression. But God forbid that she should go through the rest of her life frightened and cowed by every man who crossed her path.

She went to the clerk's window. "Are there any letters for Mrs. Lillian Courtney?"

He went to look and returned with something in his hand. "There is one."

"Thank you."

Unwilling to wait to read her letter, she went to a quiet corner in the little room, as she was its sole occupant, and tore it open.

It was from her friend Anne.

Dearest Lillian,

Forgive me, but I know of no lodgings that you might take. When Father returns from London, I shall ask him. Perhaps he will know of something. I am terribly sorry for the loss of your husband and for your reduced circumstances. Please accept my best wishes for your health and happiness.

Your Faithful Friend,

Anne S.

Lillian's heart sank at receiving such a short, cool-sounding letter from someone she'd considered her closest friend since childhood. She could only hope that Anne would indeed ask her father and that he would know of something for her, or that one of her other letters would yield something more helpful.

A tall, well-dressed man came into the post office while she was reading her letter. He wore a long cloak and a hat pulled low over his face, and he was holding a large, brown-paper-wrapped bundle in his arms. He leaned into the window and spoke so quietly to the clerk that Lillian could not hear what he was saying.

She stuffed the letter in her pocket and stepped out onto the street.

The man who had followed her ducked down a side street.

Gritting her teeth, she turned and strode straight

toward him. She'd now seen him three times, if indeed it was the same man on the Isle of Wight and here, and it was time for him to explain himself. If he had been sent to watch her by her mother-in-law, she would discover it.

The man looked startled when she came around the corner. But his startled look quickly turned hard as he narrowed his eyes at her.

"What do you mean, following me?" she demanded, pent-up rage giving a strange edge to her voice and causing her to ball her hands into fists. "Who are you? What are you doing? Did someone hire you to watch me?"

The man took a step toward her and grabbed her around the throat.

She tried to scream but he had closed off her breath. She clawed at his hand as he stared with bloodshot eyes into hers, so close she could see the red veins against his white eyeballs.

"I will slit your throat," he rasped, "if you tell anyone about me."

"What is the meaning of this?" The tall man from the post office grabbed the fiend's arm. "Unhand her."

Her aggressor let go of her throat and struck out at the tall man, who dodged to avoid the fist aimed at his chin. The tall man quickly stepped in front of Lillian.

Her throat hurt and she gasped for air. She peeked around her rescuer's side, terror still coursing through her limbs, as she stared at the man who had choked her.

"You stay right here while I call the constable," the tall gentleman said to their assailant.

The man ran past them, and then he disappeared around the corner.

Lillian wrapped her arms around herself. The man was gone. But her heart still beat hard and fast inside her chest.

"Are you all right?" Her rescuer's face was familiar. She could not remember who he was, but she'd seen him before.

"That man assaulted me," she said, her voice shaking, her thoughts jumbled. "He was following me and then he grabbed me."

"He must be some kind of fiend to lay hands on a lady. I shall notify the constable at once. But first, let's get you home. Where do you live?"

"At Stokemont Abbey."

"Ah." His expression changed. "You are Mrs. Courtney, are you not? Forgive me. I am—"

"Lord Barrentine. Yes, of course. I did not recognize you at first." He was Nash Golding, the Earl of Barrentine, of whom her husband had been so jealous.

She could never really understand why he was jealous, as her husband was just as rich and would not have liked having a title, as it would have required him to spend a great deal of time in Parliament, instead of doing just as he pleased.

"Did you walk here? I shall take you home in my carriage."

She was still shaking rather badly after being throttled by that evil man. "Thank you. That is very kind of you."

How embarrassing, to have to be rescued on the street by an earl! How mortifying, that he'd had to put himself out to help her. Although, truthfully, she didn't know why she felt embarrassed or guilty. She had done nothing wrong, and she was so grateful for the man's help. Something more horrible might have happened if he hadn't been there. And she might have been killed.

"Are you sure you are well?"

"Yes, only a bit shaken."

"Did you know the man?"

"No, not at all, but I had seen him watching me before. Although I can't imagine why."

"I am very glad you are unhurt. And please allow me to express my condolences on the death of your husband," Lord Barrentine said softly, a pained look on his face. "It must have been a great shock."

"Yes, it was. And I thank you." Inexplicably, the thought went through her head that his was the sincerest expression of condolence and compassion she'd received since her husband's death.

He escorted her down the street toward a carriage, but the black conveyance bore no coat of arms on the side. Indeed, it was a rather nondescript carriage, not the sort of vehicle she'd expect of an earl. Perhaps he wished to travel without being noticed.

"You are not so near your home, unless I misjudge the distance."

"This village is not very near, no, but I had business here."

She almost asked him, "At the post office?" but that would sound intrusive. She was no gossip, after all. But truly, it was strange that an earl would have any cause for entering a post office. He would have servants and even couriers to take care of any such business.

"You were taking your early morning walk to the village, I imagine. You said you had seen that man before, but you don't know who he is?"

"I don't know him, but I had seen him on two other occasions, unless I am mistaken, on the Isle of Wight. I do believe he has been following me and watching me, although I know that sounds strange of me to say. It is not as though it could be a coincidence that he was also on the Isle of Wight at the same time that I was staying there, I should not think."

"That is very curious indeed. Do you know of anyone who would wish to harm you?"

How much should she tell him of her mother-in-law's ire toward her? "I know of no one who has cause to harm me," she said carefully. "However, my mother-in-law, Mrs. Courtney, has no great love for me." She smiled, as if to make light of the fact, to turn it into a joke.

She really should not have said that. But Lord Barrentine was giving her an intense stare, his brows lowering in concern.

"I am terribly sorry to hear that. Do you have relatives with whom you might live? Widows, I know, are often set adrift . . . Forgive me if I am intruding on your privacy. I don't wish to pry."

"As a matter of fact, I am in search of lodgings for myself and my young daughter. Would you happen to know of any place?"

Truly, she should not ask for his help. He was barely even an acquaintance, not related to her, and he was an unmarried gentleman. But she was only asking if he knew of a place. She must sound desperate, but since she was rather desperate, so be it.

"I know Thurgood Hall is available to let."

"I could never hope to afford such a grand estate. I'm afraid my means are greatly reduced."

He chewed his bottom lip and looked deep in thought. "Allow me to inquire of my steward and my solicitor, discreetly, of course. I daresay I shall have a list of places within a week or two."

"You are so very kind." Indeed, the breath rushed out of her and she had to swallow and catch her breath at his graciousness. Could he be so kind? Could he not want something in return? Indeed, it had been so long since anyone had been so disinterestedly kind and concerned for her. Even her husband and her own brother had not been this kind.

"It is nothing at all. Is there a preference of location?"

"I should like something that is near enough to Stokemont Abbey that Mrs. Courtney could see her granddaughter often, but not so near that she would visit every day."

"I quite understand."

"Forgive me for being so candid."

"Not at all. I understand."

He really did seem as if he did not judge her. How refreshing.

Lillian still felt guilty for asking his help. If it were known, and if the wrong people presented it in a harsh light, his helping her could even tarnish his reputation. But as she'd already acknowledged, at least to herself, that she was desperate, she just prayed, *Forgive me, God, and don't allow his reputation to be harmed because of me.*

"I want you to know, you have my undying gratitude for defending me from that man. I don't know what would have happened if you had not intervened."

Her stomach did a strange little flip-flop as she remembered how he had stepped between her and her assailant. How brave he had looked, without fear in standing up to that evil man.

"It was my pleasure to come to your aid, Mrs. Courtney. And I shall notify the constable as soon as I leave here."

The carriage was already stopping at the door of Stokemont Abbey.

"I suppose the constable will wish to speak to me."

"I imagine so."

"Thank you again." She didn't want to be inconsiderate of his time, but she was strangely reluctant to leave him. Still, she had no reason not to go when the coachman opened the door to hand her out.

"Farewell, Mrs. Courtney," he said, just before the door was shut and she could no longer see him.

As she entered the house, she ruminated on how she'd seen Lord Barrentine many times at balls and assemblies, as they both resided principally in Gloucestershire—both before his father died, when he was the Viscount Holbrooke, and when he inherited the title of earl. But she'd never noticed just how handsome he was, with his brown hair and unassuming countenance. He'd always seemed slightly awkward when he danced, and she noted he was quiet in crowds, and that was all she really knew of him.

But now she also knew that he was brave and courteous, kind and chivalrous.

Well, she would see just how kind he was, and if he would indeed prove to be a man of his word, as he'd promised to help her find lodgings.

He certainly didn't owe her any help, and reputations had come into question over just such a thing as helping a widow secure lodgings. *Please, God, let him help me find something.*

After all, no one else was offering their help.

~ ~ ~

The constable arrived, unfortunately, just as Mrs.

Courtney was coming down the stairs to take her breakfast. And the exact moment the servant told Mrs. Courtney that the constable was there over an incident in the village, her eyes turned sharp and narrow, and she hurried down to join him and Lillian in the sitting room.

The constable questioned her thoroughly on what her attacker did and what he looked like.

"He had no particularly distinguishing features. He was of medium height, perhaps an inch taller than I am. His teeth were crooked and yellow, none missing that I could see, though one tooth in front was broken in half at an angle. I could smell liquor on him, and his eyes were bloodshot."

Her heart sank. He sounded like most men one might meet on the street, except, perhaps, for the broken tooth. Little good this description would do in finding the man.

"So the man you saw on the Isle of Wight may or may not have been this same man."

"I suppose that is true, but I believe it was the same man."

"But why would such a man follow you?" Mrs. Courtney inserted, letting her mouth hang open, looking as if she might laugh. "It cannot be the same man, to be both on the Isle of Wight and then to come to our little corner of Gloucestershire." Mrs. Courtney's expression was only appropriate to give to a small child—chiding and condescending.

Lillian refused to agree with her. The woman was trying to discredit her in front of the constable. After all, Lillian was the one she despised and blamed for her son's death.

"Leastways, it seems we have a man here in our

little village who doesn't shrink from attacking ladies on the street, and we cannot have that. I shall ask around and have the watchmen keep an eye out for the blighter."

"Thank you." Lillian let Mrs. Courtney see the man out.

"Well, now, and it was Lord Barrentine who came to your aid," Mrs. Courtney said, coming back into the room. Lillian tried and failed to read the woman's expression.

"Thankfully, yes."

"And you were just out for a walk, were you?"

"Yes." She'd omitted the fact that she'd gone to the post office when she described the event to the constable.

"A woman is not safe alone these days, it would seem," Mrs. Courtney said. "You must be dreadfully shaken up over it. A strange man putting his hands on you! Such a dreadful business. If such a thing happened to me, I wouldn't sleep for weeks."

What was the woman getting at? Of course, Lillian was under no delusion that Mrs. Courtney felt compassion for her.

"I am so relieved that you and Isabella are under my roof again, safe here at Stokemont Abbey."

The sharp look that shot Lillian's way told her that the woman was scheming, or at least trying to manipulate her. But Lillian would not reveal her plans to move away, not until she had found lodgings.

"I suppose you might wish to stay here at Stokemont Abbey, but I'm afraid it is no longer under my control. As you know, my son and his wife have inherited the estate. Edgar and Fanny will be taking possession very soon—by early next week, he has just informed me. I imagine you shall wish to go and live with your brother and his wife. Are they in Hampshire now?"

"Yes." Lillian's stomach sank as her face heated.

"So you will want to stay with your brother, and little Isabella can stay here under our protection—we have several male servants, after all. I am comforted by little Isabella, as the pain of losing my son is heavy and ever present. I suppose you can understand that. And the world is such a dangerous place." She punctuated this speech with a dramatic sigh.

Lillian no longer had to wonder about her mother-in-law's goal. She would use the incident to ignite Lillian's fear so that she would leave Bella at Stokemont Abbey with Mrs. Courtney while going to live with her brother.

"I will visit my brother, Christopher Hartman, in Hampshire," she said, "but I will be taking Isabella with me."

If a look could be violent, Mrs. Courtney's glare certainly would have been deadly. Lillian would not tell her of her plan to find lodgings elsewhere, but Mrs. Courtney would discover soon enough just how determined Lillian was to keep her child with her.

She braced for what Mrs. Courtney might say, but she was saved by George and Bella toddling into the room, accompanied by their respective nurses.

"There are my little angels!" Mrs. Courtney cried out. She held out her arms. "Come to Grandmamma!"

George looked resigned, almost dazed, and he went into the woman's outstretched arms, while Bella ran straight to Lillian.

"Isabella, come. Come here with me and your cousin George. Give your Grandmamma a morning hug."

Bella slowly unclasped her arms, which were around Lillian's neck, and went to her grandmother, still clutching her ragged doll tightly in her other hand. She allowed her grandmother to pick her up and set her on her knee. The woman clasped her tightly, holding George close to her other side.

"I don't know what I would do without my two precious ones."

She held Bella a little too long and too tightly, for she started squirming to get down.

"Your mother doesn't need you," she said. "Stay with me."

But Bella struggled all the more to get down. Finally, Mrs. Courtney let her go, and she ran to Lillian.

Mrs. Courtney was giving Lillian an even colder glare than before.

"Well, then, George and I shall go find some breakfast, something sweet, I daresay. Some cake?" She bent to look George in the eye. "You would like cake for breakfast. I shall send for some, and if there is none, we shall have Cook make your favorite cake."

And she left the room with George holding onto her hand.

A shudder passed through Lillian's shoulders, as Mrs. Courtney had just reminded her so much of her and her brother Christopher's old nurse, who used to try to make them jealous of each other in order to manipulate them.

She shuddered again and held Bella close.

CHAPTER FOUR

After saving Mrs. Courtney from the ruffian's attack, Nash had gone straight to the constable's home and spoke to him about what had happened in the village. Then he went home and asked his steward and solicitor to discreetly inquire about lodgings that Courtney's widow might be able to afford.

Three days later, he sat poring over the list of choices they had given him.

They had found only a few options, and none of them seemed quite right. They were either too costly for her means—his solicitor actually knew how much her father had settled on her, whereas her husband had died without a will and she had inherited nothing from his estate—or they were in some other way unsuitable.

The more he thought about it, the more he wanted to offer her the dowager cottage behind his estate.

The cottage belonged to him, but he should probably speak to his mother before offering it. And truthfully, he felt it his duty to find out more about this Lillian Courtney first.

She was quite beautiful, he couldn't help thinking, when he got a better look at her after stopping the evil man from strangling her. And the more he thought about it, the more he wished he had hit that man in the face with his fist. But it was obvious the man was drunk. A hard shove would have probably knocked him over.

Normally Nash would have felt inept around such a beautiful woman, but she had been in such great need, and seemed so thankful for his help, he somehow forgot to feel his usual awkwardness. He felt as if he were in one of the novels that he often satirized, rescuing a lady in distress. Such things didn't actually happen in England, or so he had thought.

He would have to rethink his assumption that such things were extremely rare or nonexistent.

Later that evening, when he was dining with his mother, his two younger sisters being at a friend's house party, he asked her, "What do you know about the Courtney family?"

"I know the death of the young Mr. Courtney has been much talked of. I've even heard that his wife left him and took the child to the Isle of Wight, and he followed her there. He managed to fall off a cliff during his first night on the island. It's all rather strange and suspicious.

"I also know that the newly deceased Mr. Courtney's mother took one of her grandchildren to raise, her daughter's child. Your sister Elizabeth is good friends with the child's mother. When Elizabeth asked her why she let her mother take her child to live with her, she said, 'Mother always gets what she wants, and if I fought her, she would win in the end and would take out her vengeance on me. I had little choice.' Or something of that nature."

"And what of the new widow? Do you know any-thing about her?"

"Not much. Why do you ask?"

Nash decided to relate all that had occurred that morning—except for why he was in that village. He had gone there precisely because it was far enough away from home, and early enough in the morning, that he wouldn't expect to meet with anyone who would recognize him. He had no wish for his mother to learn that he was mailing his newest manuscript off to his publisher in London.

He told his mother about intervening when the stranger accosted the young Mrs. Lillian Courtney.

"How perfectly dreadful! I'm so glad neither of you were injured."

"Mrs. Courtney did ask my assistance on the way to her home in my coach."

"Assistance?"

"Yes. She has a small annual sum that her father settled on her, which is all she has to live on, and she wishes to find lodgings for herself and her daughter. She asked if I might know of any suitable place. I told her I would inquire for her."

"Why does she not live at Stokemont Abbey? I'm sure Mrs. Courtney would be happy to have them stay there."

"After what you just told me, perhaps Lillian Court-ney fears her mother-in-law would rather have the child and not her under her roof. Besides, will it not be her hus-band's brother who will inherit Stokemont Abbey? Per-haps she will not feel welcome for that reason as well."

"Yes, of course. You are right. Did you find any pos-sible lodgings for her? There is the old Bishop Hill Lodge."

"She could never afford Bishop Hill Lodge."

"Or Deerwood Hall?"

"Again, well beyond her means."

"Darling, I suspect you are thinking of having her stay in our dowager cottage. Is that what you are thinking?"

"I was thinking of it as a possibility."

"Darling, you know we do not wish to cross Mrs. Courtney. That lady holds grudges. You remember how she ruined that young man who represented Gloucestershire in the House of Commons. She shredded his reputation, though he had done nothing to deserve it, solely because her daughter felt rejected by him when he did not wish to marry her. Do you remember?"

"Yes, Mother, I remember. Are you saying we should be too afraid of her to be of service to a young lady in need, solely because Mrs. Courtney will not like it?"

"Son, I know what an idealist you are, but you must listen to reason."

"I am listening."

Mother stared out the window for several long moments. "Very well. I shall invite her to dine with us, but I shall have to invite the older Mrs. Courtney to dine as well, or it will look suspicious."

He would much rather not invite old Mrs. Courtney to dine with them, but perhaps seeing them together would add insight.

~ ~ ~

Four days later, early in the morning, Lillian walked toward the village of Gantt on her way to the post office, even though she was very frightened. Indeed, the closer she came, the harder her heart beat, becoming painful. She nearly turned back. But she would not allow one evil man to control her. She clenched her teeth and continued on.

She kept a keen eye out for the man who had accosted her as she made her way through the village and entered the post office. There was only one letter, and unfortunately, it was another friend saying she did not know of any lodgings for her.

Taking several deep breaths and telling herself that she would not be frightened, as the constable was looking for her assailant and would no doubt have scared him away, Lillian finally stepped out onto the street. She glanced all around before assuring herself that the man was not in sight, and she walked quickly back toward Stokemont Abbey to prepare to leave with Bella the next morning to visit Christopher and Gretchen.

An hour later, she was breaking her fast with Mrs. Courtney when the servant handed her mother-in-law the letters. Mrs. Courtney was reading them when she looked up.

"We have been invited," Mrs. Courtney said.

"Invited?" Lillian prompted.

"To dine at Dunbridge Hall Friday next."

Lillian must have looked confused, because Mrs. Courtney gave her a stern look.

"Dunbridge Hall? The family estate of the Earl of Barrentine? It must be a dinner party, but since Edgar and Fanny will already be here, I cannot imagine why they would only invite you and I. Perhaps they do not know that Edgar and Fanny will be here."

Lillian was a bit confused as well. She had as good as told Lord Barrentine that she was trying to find a place away from Mrs. Courtney, to get away from her. She prayed he wouldn't mention that she was looking for lodgings in front of Mrs. Courtney. Perhaps she could catch him alone for a moment to ask him not to. But Friday next seemed such a long time away. She'd be in Hampshire then with her brother. She probably would not even be able to attend, but she said nothing of it to Mrs. Courtney.

~ ~ ~

Lillian requested the carriage that had so recently been her own to take her to Christopher's house. Mrs. Courtney granted her request, looking down her nose, her eyelids nearly closed, as if she were granting a magnanimous favor to someone who was far from deserving.

Mrs. Courtney mumbled, "It is a very great expense. Hampshire is a long way, and to be taking my grand-daughter away from me."

But as she only mumbled the remark, turning her head away, Lillian knew she wasn't meant to acknowledge the comments or to make any reply. So she did not.

Lillian made sure to pack all her belongings, leaving nothing behind that was solely hers, but also taking nothing that would be considered as belonging to the house or to her late husband. In the end, Mrs. Courtney did not see them off or say good-bye to Bella.

Could Mrs. Courtney be contemplating leaving them alone, giving up on her wish to have Bella to herself? Lillian should not get her hopes up, but she couldn't help hoping anyway.

On the carriage ride, she tried to prepare herself to be in the company of her brother and Gretchen. She also sang songs and recited nursery rhymes with Bella trying to keep her child occupied. Mostly, Bella occupied herself with a constant sing-song way of voicing her thoughts and commentary as she stared out the window at the passing countryside.

"Pretty, pretty flowers and grass," she sang, to no particular tune. "There's a hill and Mamma could take me there. We would have tea and eat cake on the grass. A pretty tree with lovely leaves," she continued in her sing-song way.

Lillian couldn't help but smile at Bella's sweet voice singing her innocent thoughts. But as she considered what might happen to them, being forced to live with either her brother or her former mother-in-law, her smile turned to tears. If she were given her way, would Mrs. Courtney turn her grandchildren into monsters just as she'd turned her son into one, through ridiculous indulgences coupled with degrading and humiliating criticism?

Lillian quickly flicked the tears away, took a deep breath, and tried to think of something else. Bella was happy, for she only sang when she was calm and happy, and Lillian would stay with her always. She'd even left the nurse at Stokemont Abbey, saying she couldn't afford to keep her, but Mrs. Courtney assured Bella that she would keep her nurse for her, that she would be there when they returned.

Lillian prayed they would never have to return.

When they arrived at her childhood home, her brother actually greeted her at the door of the large manor house their father had bought when they were small children. He and Mother had been dead for five and twelve years, respectively, so she associated Christopher with the house more than anyone else. And Gretchen, since he married her five years before.

"Hey, sis. I'm as sorry as I can be about Courtney's death. What a shame," her brother said, interjecting a curse word here and there, which was his way.

It was the first she'd heard of his sorrow. Neither he nor his wife had written to her. But she did appreciate how sincere he sounded.

"Thank you."

"This one has grown." He patted Bella's shoulder.

"This is your Uncle Christopher," Lillian said to Bella, who cringed a bit at the stranger patting her.

"I've got a little girl who will be glad to see you." Christopher looked behind him.

"Let them in, Christopher." Gretchen's voice sounded annoyed. "Don't keep them standing at the door."

Christopher stepped back. Gretchen was leading a nurse who was carrying a child of about two years old, who must have been their daughter, Priscilla.

Priscilla looked so small, as Lillian was used to seeing Bella, who was a year older. Priscilla's hair was white-blonde and wispy, her blue eyes big and round.

Bella reached a tentative hand toward her little cousin. Priscilla immediately started crying.

"Priscilla, don't cry. This is your cousin, Bella." Christopher nudged his daughter, then patted her on the back.

"I'm sure they'll become good friends when they've had more time together." Lillian spoke calmly, knowing how quickly her brother could become frustrated. "All is well."

Gretchen finally came forward and gave Lillian an awkward embrace from the side. "It's so terrible what happened. I don't know how you can be holding up. Such a tragic thing to happen, your husband dying so young, and in such a way." Gretchen's eyes were sharp as she stared at Lillian, who saw no compassion in her expression.

"Yes. It was sudden."

"Well, you are welcome here, of course." But it was the ironic tone in which Gretchen said the words that made her wonder if she meant just the opposite.

A servant showed them to their room as their things were carried in. Bella had begun to suck on her thumb, a sure sign that she was sleepy, and while Lillian supervised the putting away of their clothing in the wardrobe, Bella fell asleep on her shoulder. Lillian laid her on the bed to sleep, then she slipped out, knowing Bella would sleep for at least an hour.

Gretchen called from the bottom of the stairs that they were taking tea, so Lillian went down and joined them.

"How are you holding up, Lillian?" Gretchen squinted and scrunched her face at Lillian.

"I am well."

"But your husband just died. You must be devastated. Christopher and I have been so worried about you and about where you will live, now that your husband is gone and left you nothing to live on."

Christopher sat staring at the wall, a glass of what smelled like brandy in his hand.

"Our father settled a small sum on me, so I was actually wondering if you would know of a place I could let for a small sum. I don't have a lot of money, but I have enough for—"

"Father settled a generous amount on you, and Grandfather left you the cottage." Christopher was still staring at the wall when he took a sip of his brandy. "You should live quite well on the Isle of Wight."

"But she is devastated, Christopher. She will not

wish to go so far away from Isabella's family. She will want to stay near Stokemont Abbey and here."

"I was hoping to stay near family. Do you know of any lodgings that might be available to let?"

"I am sure we can make inquiries." Gretchen smiled, as if eager to be of help.

"It will have to be very modest," Lillian said, trying to sound as if she did not mind at all, wishing she had not mentioned her need of lodgings in front of Gretchen.

"Oh? How modest?" Gretchen's eyes, again, gave her quite a sharp look. "I am sure we can find something. Isn't that so, Christopher?"

There was no indication that he had even heard her question for several moments. Finally, he said, "I shall see what I can find."

"Please don't trouble yourselves," Lillian said, still trying to make light of her situation. "I am sure something will turn up. I do not wish to intrude on anyone, but I believe I will find something—"

"I'll have Stratford search for something. Is there any particular area you wanted?"

"I'd like something close enough to Stokemont Abbey that Mrs. Courtney will not be angry that I took Bella too far away from her."

"Oh, yes, that is very good thinking indeed," Gretchen gushed. "She will need her granddaughter near her so that she will not miss her son so much. It must be such a trial for her as well as you. Such a sudden, shocking death. Does Bella miss her father terribly? She probably cries for him. Such a sad, sad thing."

"Well, it is not so sad as all that," Lillian said quietly, even as a warning in her head told her to tread carefully and not reveal too much.

Christopher's eyes were finally trained on Lillian. They were both waiting for her to go on.

"I only mean that my husband was not very attentive to his daughter, and I do not believe she misses him. And I do not miss him either, as he was neither kind nor loving to me."

"He didn't . . ." Christopher cleared his throat. "Didn't strike you, did he?"

"He did. And that is why I am not sad he's gone." But even as she said the words, tears threatened to spill from her eyes. She took a deep breath to dispel them.

Christopher mumbled some curses in a hushed tone. "If he was still alive . . . I wish I'd known, sis." He cursed again, then repeated, "I wish I'd known."

"It is all right. He is gone now so it doesn't matter."

"You poor thing," Gretchen said. "To think you were being mistreated. Poor Isabella. Well, now you can find your own place and not have to worry about being struck by your husband."

Gretchen began to talk on and on about her own family. She told a story about her father beating her with a riding crop until she had bloody stripes on her back and arms that bled through her dress. She told the story as if it was a normal event and nothing out of the ordinary, and she spoke without pause and seemed to wish for no comment from anyone.

"But if my husband were to strike me . . . Christopher is very good to me, as you know, I'm sure. He has never struck me, never. In fact, just the other day . . ."

Lillian stopped listening. She suddenly felt weary to her bones—and desperate to get away from Gretchen's voice, which seemed to grate on her nerves like the unceasing scream of a peacock.

She waited for a lull in Gretchen's voice, but she waited in vain, for when Gretchen finished one story about her childhood, she immediately began another without even a pause.

Finally, Lillian stood up. Another few moments and Gretchen finally said, "Are you tired from your journey? Of course you are. You will want to go to your room and change and freshen up. I suppose Isabella is with her nurse. They can take a walk around the gardens if they—"

"I did not bring Isabella's nurse, and yes, I am tired. I will go and take a nap with Bella."

"We'll see you at dinner," Christopher said. He walked her to the stairs, then said quietly, "I wish you had told me about Courtney." He cursed him, then said, "I would have taught him better, if I'd known. I'm glad you're rid of him."

Lillian simply nodded. "Thank you for letting Bella and me visit."

"Of course. You're welcome here any time."

But even her brother must realize that she wouldn't want to stay indefinitely.

CHAPTER FIVE

Lillian awoke on their third day at her brother's house with Bella asleep beside her. She prayed, quite hopelessly, *Please help me find somewhere for us to live.*

If worse came to worse, she could go live at her grandfather's cottage, but that seemed a great risk, besides the fact that she knew no one there.

But she should not pray such hopeless prayers. God was not pleased with a lack of faith. But God also understood, surely, that she was doing the best she could. After three days of listening to Gretchen's endless talking and stories, she was worn and weary, like a scrubby tree on the moor, so harassed by the wind that it was only a tenth of its normal height and size.

When Bella opened her eyes and said, "I'm hungry," Lillian got them both dressed and went down to the breakfast room.

As they neared the open door, Lillian didn't hear her sister-in-law's voice. Could it be that they would not have to see her while they ate breakfast? Lillian held her breath as they approached the doorway.

"I was beginning to wonder if you two were awake." Gretchen hardly took a breath as she began to regale them with a story of Priscilla and her father taking a walk and coming upon a badger fighting with a poisonous adder. As with all her stories, she told it as if it were nothing out of the ordinary. Immediately after that story, she told a story of her mother, who thought it was a good lesson for her, when she broke her leg, to force her to walk on it as punishment for jumping off a haystack after she'd told her not to.

"I did disobey her, but when my brother did the same thing two years later, she had the servants carry him all the way back to the house, and his leg wasn't even broken, as it turned out. But she always treated him differently, I suppose because he was her youngest child and she favored him over the rest of us. She always said he was an easier child than I was, and I'm sure she would have left their estate to him instead of my eldest brother, if she could."

Lillian wanted to say she was sorry her mother had treated her that way. When Lillian had first met Gretchen, immediately after her wedding to Christopher, she often expressed alarm and sympathy over these stories that Gretchen told about her parents' treatment of her, but it was as if her sister-in-law didn't comprehend what she was saying and did not receive the sentiments. And though she spoke so often of her parents' mistreatment, never once did she acknowledge that the treatment was vile or in any way wrong. So Lillian had learned to listen to the horrendous stories and refrain from commenting —most of the time. There were times when she could not help herself.

"Is Christopher at home today?"

"I believe he went for a ride. He said he might not be home until sometime tomorrow, if he went to Andrew Hitchcock's to play cards tonight."

Lillian's heart sank. She'd hoped to speak to him again about how he might help her find lodgings for herself and Bella. She was anxious to find a place, as soon as possible.

She did her best to smile cheerfully at Bella and encourage her to eat, as Bella was talking to her doll instead of eating.

"Aren't you hungry, darling?"

Bella shook her head and went on telling her doll, "If you are good, Mamma shall take us on a walk in the garden. You would like that."

"Priscilla should be here soon, when she wakes up and gets dressed. She's so slow. She's more like an eighty-year-old than a two-year-old."

"I don't like to be rushed when I first wake up either." Lillian tried to sound and look compassionate. The poor woman probably had no idea how to treat her child with compassion, after her own horrific childhood. Lillian only hoped Priscilla's nurse was kind and understanding with her.

~ ~ ~

A few days later, Lillian had just come from the nursery less than half an hour before and settled in the sitting room to read a book. The nurse was watching the two children, who were playing together. From Lillian's observation, the nurse was a kindhearted and attentive girl, barely seventeen years old, who had had some education in the work house where she spent most of her childhood. Lillian was overcautious, as her mother-in-law and husband had often told her, and she had watched the nurse interact with the children until she was satisfied, having seen no signs of hostility or ill temper in her.

"There you are." Gretchen strode into the room and began to talk of the weather, then how lazy her servants were. Lillian set her book aside.

"Have you heard from Christopher?" Lillian said, interrupting her sister-in-law.

"Not for two days now, but that is his way. He goes to play cards or shoot with his friends. That is how men are. Once my father didn't come home for twenty-one days, and my mother did not hear a word from him all that time. When he did come home—"

They heard shouts and went to the window and watched as Christopher fell off his horse, flat on his face and stomach. He did not move, while a groom standing next him shouted for help.

"Christopher must be sick," Lillian said. "Shouldn't we go down to him?"

With a slightly amused smirk, Gretchen said, "No, he's only drunk too much brandy. He comes home like this quite often. He's not an angry drunk, at least. He just gets sleepier and sleepier. Once—I wish you could have seen him—he fell asleep at the table. His face fell right into his plate and he didn't even wake up." She laughed.

Lillian's stomach twisted as she watched the grooms, on the front lawn, rouse Christopher enough to get him on his feet, and then two of them wrapped his arms around their shoulders and half carried, half dragged him inside.

O God, please help my poor brother.

Gretchen went with the grooms as they carried him through the hall toward the stairs.

"Let us get him to bed where he can sleep until

sometime tomorrow."

At least Gretchen seemed to take great care of her husband, even though she had gone all day without seeing her child. "The nurse is with her. She doesn't need me," Gretchen had said more than once since Lillian and Bella had arrived.

A minute after Gretchen and the grooms had disappeared upstairs, Lillian saw a rider galloping up the lane.

The servant came moments later and said, "There's a courier at the door. He has a letter for you, ma'am."

"For me?" Lillian took the letter.

"Yes, ma'am, and he is waiting for your answer."

The letter was from Lord Barrentine's mother, asking if they might send their carriage to her, to bring her to their home for the dinner party they'd invited her and Mrs. Courtney to, keep her overnight, then have their carriage take her home the next day.

Her heart contracted inside her chest at the thought of being away from Bella for more than twenty-four hours.

We are very happy, her letter said, *to provide transportation, as Mrs. Courtney says you have gone to visit your brother. Please say yes, as we wish to tell you of the possible lodgings we have found for you.*

This last sentence eased her heart. And since it did not seem as if she could rely on her brother's help, she quickly wrote her answer at the bottom of the letter and gave it to the courier.

In one more day, she would at least get a short respite from the heaviness she felt in being with her brother and his wife. And she must not worry about Bella. She would be safe with Priscilla's nurse, and they might have new lodgings to retreat to very soon.

~ ~ ~

Dunbridge Hall was an impressive, castle-like structure, with towers and turrets. It was made of local stone, but looked as though it had been built more recently than most English castles, in the last two hundred years. There were more windows than the average castle, which meant it would be less dark, which Lillian could appreciate.

Lord Barrentine looked quite a bit less awkward than he did at parties, as he greeted his guests with his mother by his side. They'd also invited a widower, Lord Gomfrey, and his son Harold, with whom Lillian was only a little acquainted.

The evening began pleasantly enough. Lord Gomfrey was an excellent conversationalist who drew out the more reticent members of the party, which were Lillian and Lord Barrentine, although Lord Barrentine was more talkative than she'd expected. When no one else was listening at dinner, he conversed quite intelligently with her about literature and architecture, which he declared were his "two favorite subjects of study" when he was at Oxford.

She indicated an interest in the history of Dunbridge Hall, and he entertained her for several minutes together. She listened so attentively that she momentarily forgot her troubles—forgot she was a widow of meager means in need of a place where she and her daughter could live without fear.

"I must be boring you tremendously," he said suddenly. "Forgive me."

"Not at all. I am very intrigued by England's great homes and castles and palaces. It is an interest of mine as well. Dunbridge Hall is a very fine structure, and I enjoy hearing about its history."

The other guests seemed to be caught up in a lively story Lord Gomfrey and his son were telling about a hunting trip gone awry, so no one was listening as she spoke as quietly as she could to Lord Barrentine.

"I wanted to thank you for coming to my aid the other day, and also to ask you not to mention what I told you about seeking lodgings."

"Of course. You may depend upon my discretion, and my mother's as well."

"I am very grateful."

"I have not forgotten my promise, and I do have a list for you, which my mother shall give to you later, privately."

When Lillian glanced across the table, she saw Mrs. Courtney watching them with a shrewd look. Had she heard what they were saying?

Lillian turned her attention on her food. She was supposed to be mourning her husband.

She probably should not have been enjoying her conversation with Lord Barrentine so much. It was true that she was rather deprived of intelligent, mutually stimulating conversation after living with her husband and mother-in-law for so long. And soon her husband's brother and his wife would move into Stokemont Abbey, and she knew them too well to think they would improve the situation.

They all retired to the drawing room, as the men professed not to like smoking after dinner.

Again, Lord Gomfrey's conversation was lively and included everyone. He seemed to instinctively know what would most interest each member of the party and changed the topic of conversation often to include everyone. Lillian could see why they had invited him, as her mother-in-law invariably turned the conversation to political controversies, and Lillian would rather be silent than mocked and judged, which Mrs. Courtney seemed eager to do.

"I can often find something to admire in the arguments of both the Tories and the Whigs," Lillian said, when Lord Gomfrey asked her opinion of a topic Mrs. Courtney introduced.

"You don't side with the Tories?" Mrs. Courtney said, looking dumbfounded. "Why, that is extraordinary, since your husband was a staunch Tory. I suppose you think you know better than your husband, that your wisdom is superior—"

Lillian's cheeks burned as she tried to think how she might defend herself. But Lord Gomfrey quickly introduced a new topic of conversation, so deftly that no one seemed to notice that Mrs. Courtney had more to say on the subject. Even Mrs. Courtney was diverted.

When the evening was over, as they waited for the carriage to be brought round, Mrs. Courtney turned to narrow her eyes at Lillian and said, "I hope you are sensible of the great favor Lord and Lady Barrentine have done in sending for you in their carriage. It is quite a long way from here to your brother's home in Hampshire, and therefore a great expense."

"I am very grateful to them for the favor," Lillian said, smiling as if to say that she did not note the coldness in her former mother-in-law's remark.

"It is nothing at all," Lady Barrentine said cheerily. "We have enjoyed her company very much and shall be more than happy to send for her again, I'm sure."

A servant came in and said something quietly to

Lord Barrentine. After a short conversation, the servant left and Lord Barrentine turned to his guests.

"I'm afraid, Mrs. Courtney, the axle on your carriage needs to be repaired. My groom saw the problem, but it can be fixed rather quickly, probably by tomorrow afternoon."

"Axle?" Mrs. Courtney said the word as if it was offensive. "The axle is broken?"

"Not broken in two, only in need of a little work, and my man can do it for you, but he is asleep now. You are welcome to stay the night."

"Yes, please stay with us tonight," Lady Barrentine said quickly. "You are most welcome."

Mrs. Courtney seemed quite shocked about the carriage axle, but she was finally persuaded to allow her carriage to be repaired the next day and to spend the night at Dunbridge Hall.

When the servant had taken Mrs. Courtney up to her room, Lady Barrentine placed her hand on Lillian's arm. "And now, my dear, I shall have the servant take you to your room in a moment, but first, I have something to discuss with you."

"Yes?"

"Here, my dear," she said, as she slipped a folded piece of paper into her hand. "This is a list of all the places we found for you, possible lodgings, but please allow us to offer you our dowager cottage, which is on our estate, at no expense to you. You are most welcome to it."

"Oh, that is so very kind of you, but I cannot possibly—that is, I must pay you something. I am most happy to pay you whatever you think it's worth."

Her heart was leaping inside her, interfering with her breathing, for she suddenly felt almost breathless.

"Truly, we are most happy to offer it. No one is living there, it has been empty for a long time, and we know you are in need. Besides, you are delightful company, and I should like to know you better."

"You are too kind."

"In the morning you can look at it and decide. For now, go and get some sleep, my dear."

"I don't know what to say. It is so very kind of you."

"Go and sleep, now."

"Thank you."

The servant had returned from showing Mrs. Courtney to her room and led Lillian up the stairs.

Could this be the answer to her prayers? But she would not allow them to give her the cottage for nothing. She would pay them what it was worth, but what a blessing, to feel so safe and protected at the Dunbridge Hall estate.

Almost as soon as the servant left and closed the door to Lillian's room, a knock came. Lillian opened the door to see Mrs. Courtney standing there.

"Will you not invite me in, or shall we talk standing here in the hall?" Mrs. Courtney said.

"Come in." Lillian carefully concealed the paper that contained the list that Lady Barrentine had given her in her hand, closing her fingers over it.

"I suppose you have made a conquest tonight," Mrs. Courtney said, her tone flat.

"I don't know what you mean, but I thought Lady Barrentine was very kind to invite us. They know we are both in mourning."

Mrs. Courtney emitted a low sound, perhaps in dispute of Lillian's words. She said nothing for several moments, then broke the silence.

"I saw you and Lord Barrentine whispering together like lovers at the table."

"I am sorry you misunderstood. Like lovers? Hardly. We are only slightly acquainted." She should not dignify Mrs. Courtney's remark with a defensive reply, but she couldn't help herself. Lovers? Why must Mrs. Courtney hate her so?

"What was Lord Barrentine doing in the village of Gantt on the day you were accosted by that man? Had you and Lord Barrentine arranged to meet there?"

"Of course not. I had never spoken to the man in my life before that day."

"Hm, well, you cannot blame me for asking. It is all very suspicious."

Lillian wanted to demand to know how it was suspicious. She fumed at the woman's cruelty and coldness. The only people who had been kind to her in a long time were Lord and Lady Barrentine.

She longed to lash out at Mrs. Courtney, but it would do no good and would only make things more awkward for her. After all, conflict did not make Mrs. Courtney uncomfortable. On the contrary, she seemed to thrive on it.

"And what was the meaning of you taking Isabella and running away to the Isle of Wight? Explain yourself. Were you trying to lure your husband there to murder him?"

Her blunt accusation took Lillian's breath away. How dare she even think such a thing? She should probably ignore her, but the words bubbled up inside her.

"I was running away from my husband because he struck me in the back, and such behavior is intolerable to me. But I had nothing to do with my husband following me there, nothing to do with his falling off a cliff. I am guilty of no crime, and you are wrong to falsely accuse me."

Mrs. Courtney said nothing, but Lillian could hear her heavy breathing. Finally, she said, "I hope you can sleep tonight after such behavior as yours tonight, flirting with another man when your husband is hardly cold in his grave." She spun around on her heel, yanked the door open, and left. Lillian had to close the door herself.

After standing there, dumbfounded, she finally opened the piece of paper from Lady Barrentine, her hands shaking slightly after her unwanted conversation with Mrs. Courtney, and sat down to read it.

Dear Mrs. Lillian Courtney, the letter began. *My son has compiled this list of possible lodgings available, with the corresponding fee.*

Below that was the list of lodgings, but the cost for each one was quite beyond her means. Then, scribbled at the bottom of the letter were the words, *Please allow us to offer you our dowager cottage.*

Lillian clasped the letter to her chest. Could they truly be so kind and generous? Her cheeks heated and she felt a bit embarrassed at the thought that she was so destitute that she would need charity. She wasn't entirely destitute. She could pay them something, but how could she accept their offer? To so intrude upon their lives as to live on their estate. No doubt the dowager cottage they spoke of was in sight of the main house. She'd be living almost as one of their family.

In spite of feeling so humbled by their offer, it was such a relief to have somewhere to go! She and Bella would not have to stay with her brother and Gretchen, nor would they be where Mrs. Courtney could do as she wished with them—controlling Bella's very life, while despising and accusing Lillian at every turn. Dunbridge Hall was the perfect distance away.

Now they could live and be free, and Mrs. Courtney could not accuse her of trying to keep Bella away from her, as they would only be twelve miles away, about two hours by carriage. And yet, Mrs. Courtney hated traveling, because the motion of a carriage often made her sick. She would not be so quick to visit them, and certainly could not come every day. She might try to force Lillian to let Bella stay with her, but Lillian would be firm. She would not allow her child to be taken from her.

"Thank you, God," she said softly. "Thank you for making a way for us." *And thank you, Lady Barrentine and Lord Barrentine.* She would never forget their kindness.

CHAPTER SIX

Nash watched Mother direct the servants as they cleaned and readied the cottage to be occupied by Lillian Courtney and her daughter.

Part of him was quite happy that he could help someone in need. After all, the Bible said that pure religion, undefiled before the Father, was to help the widows and orphans in their distress. And it felt good to know that he had fulfilled a need for someone who seemingly had no one else to turn to.

Nevertheless, there was another part of him that was uncomfortable with the idea of helping a young unmarried woman. What if someone tried to use it against him? If he were married and settled, and if he did not worry about bringing down his party and causing problems in Parliament, he wouldn't care what anyone said. But he also did not wish to have a stranger—for Lillian Courtney was basically a stranger to him—living so near. What if she discovered his secret? Or she began to think of him as a marriage prospect? He didn't wish to have another situation on his hands like the incident with Miss

Henrietta Caldwell.

Miss Caldwell had called on him numerous times when he was forced to be in London while Parliament was in session, all because he danced with her twice at a ball. Apparently, in her mind, dancing with someone more than once in a night was tantamount to an engagement. And when she'd finally forced him to be frank with her, she said he'd broken her heart and burst into tears.

Never had he been more uncomfortable. He had been on the verge of asking her to marry him just to make her stop crying. But his father, who was still alive then, had previously told him to think of what he'd be saddled with in marrying a girl like her. She might be upset now, but marrying her would not keep her from being upset later.

There had even been a mild scandal when the girl went around telling her friends and family that Nash had broken off their engagement. There had never been an engagement. Nothing of the kind was ever spoken of or, indeed, even thought of by him. But he refused to make any accusations against her. In the end, the entire thing had caused him so much embarrassment, he had vowed never to dance again.

Of course, he did go back to dancing at balls, but he would never again dance with a lady more than once in a night, unless he was married to her.

Lillian Courtney, of course, seemed much more sensible than Henrietta Caldwell had been. She was also more beautiful, but it would be quite unusual—and much talked about—if he, an earl and a viscount who had never married and was barely twenty-five, should marry a widow with a child.

He sighed. He'd never thought of himself as a coward. After all, as a young man in boarding school, he never backed down from a fight. Fighting bullies caused the other fellows to respect you. But in adulthood, gossip-mongers had made him something of a coward—gossips and ladies who wanted to marry him.

He would be able to judge the situation better to-morrow, for that was when the widow would arrive with her daughter.

He'd expressed to his mother, gently and in a subdued manner, his concerns with having the young woman living on their estate.

"Do not worry," Mother had told him. "You won't even have to see her if you don't wish. I shall take care of everything."

"It seems unfair for you to take on the burden when it was my doing."

"Burden? I don't believe Mrs. Lillian Courtney will be any burden. She seems perfectly sweet and amiable, even a little beaten down by life's worries and a belliger-ent mother-in-law."

He hoped his mother was right.

He went back to his desk and to his new story, which he had just started writing that morning, about a poor but beautiful young widow who is kidnapped by an evil Italian count and must be rescued by a dashing and fearless English earl. But in order to poke fun at the popular novels of the day, he would have to twist the plot in some way—have the kidnapped widow become the vil-lain, perhaps. In the end, the Italian count could turn out to be the victim of the young widow, and he and the Eng-lish earl could be the heroes who lock her up in Newgate Prison.

That ending didn't exactly fill him with excited anticipation. He'd have to keep working on it.

~ ~ ~

Lillian reminded herself, *I'm doing this for Bella*, as they rode toward Dunbridge Hall.

They needed a home away from Mrs. Courtney, a place away from that lady's smothering attention. But she was also tremendously relieved to be putting so much distance between herself and her brother and his wife.

"I'm glad Lord Barrentine found a place for you," Christopher had said. "He's rich enough, and if you can get him, he'd be a good husband."

"What makes you say that?" Lillian was curious about his thought process.

"He's an earl and he's rich," Christopher answered, as if her question was silly.

But Lillian had learned the hard way that when choosing a husband, riches and position in society meant nothing.

"You will like it here, Bella," she said softly, as her daughter was very quiet and held her doll close. "We will be very happy and shall have tea parties every day."

It was difficult to take so much help from people who were of no relation and of whom she knew so little and such a short time. But was the difficulty because of misplaced pride, an unwillingness to accept help or to admit she needed help? Or was it because she was afraid to trust them?

She suspected it was more the latter.

She wished she could trust her brother and his wife, but there were many reasons why she did not. She'd also learned she couldn't trust her own father, for he had nearly bankrupted the family before his death due to a secret affinity for gambling. And her husband, on whom she'd placed all her hopes for the future, had turned out to be the most untrustworthy person of all, treating her with contempt and a complete lack of love. So perhaps it was little wonder she struggled to trust that Lord Barrentine and his mother had no unscrupulous motives for inviting her to stay in their cottage.

God, show me what to think. Keep Bella and me safe, and let me not be ungrateful for any gift of yours.

Lady Barrentine greeted her and Bella as they departed their carriage, which was loaded with all of their personal possessions.

She then introduced the housekeeper and butler and sent the carriage around the main house to the cottage so the male servants could carry their things inside.

"Please do take tea with me first, and then I shall show you the cottage."

Lillian thanked her and spoke cheerfully to cover up her nervous feelings. "You are so very kind. I thank you, Lady Barrentine, on behalf of myself and my daughter, for allowing us the use of the cottage. We are so grateful for your kindness. But I do insist upon paying you what it's worth."

"You are most welcome to the cottage, my dear. No one is using it, nor are they likely to for a long, long time. Let us have pleasant conversation just now. And this is Isabella?" She raised her brows at Bella, who gazed back at her in silence.

"Her name is Isabella, but I call her Bella."

"Bella, you shall come and have tea with me often, will you not?"

"We are at your service, Lady Barrentine."

"Please, call me Amelia. I dislike formality at home."

"Then you must call me Lillian."

"Lillian and Bella. I like those names. Now, let us go have our tea."

While they ate biscuits and sipped their tea, and Bella had her cup of milk, Lady Barrentine—Lillian simply could not call her Amelia—asked, "Will Bella have a nurse?"

"I'm afraid I cannot afford a nurse at present, but I am happy to watch her myself."

Lady Barrentine looked startled. After a moment, she said, "If you don't have to pay for lodging, would you be able to have a nurse?"

"Well, yes, but I do not wish to—"

"Now, now, we shall talk it over with Nash tonight and the two of us shall convince you, and then you can hire a nurse for the child."

"Truly, I would rather not hire a nurse. I like the idea of just the two of us in the cottage."

Lady Barrentine was quiet for a moment, and Lillian wondered if she had offended her. But she was not sorry for making her intentions clear. It was better to settle things now, at the beginning, instead of having misunderstandings later.

"Many people have told me that I'm overprotective, and they say I will make Bella into a nervous child by not leaving her care to a nurse, but I want to make certain she is properly cared for. She is my only child, as you know."

"Truthfully, I was the same way with my children," Lady Barrentine said. "I did not wish them to be without their mother all day every day. Although it is not a popular sentiment, it seemed unnatural to me to leave my children's care completely to someone unrelated to them. I did actually keep a rather close eye on them."

"Then you think as I do." Lillian's spirit lifted.

"Children are a delight, and they do not stay young and sweet for long. Sometimes I quite miss my children being Bella's age." She sighed, her eyes misting over, as she watched Bella play with her doll. "I can see she is not much trouble—quiet and easy to manage. Boys are much harder, I assure you. And you have been through a shock, and having to leave your home . . . well, I can understand your feelings. Perhaps it will be good for you to have a peaceful, quiet home with no servants. But I do hope you will dine with us often. With my children quite grown up, they are often away. Nash has only just returned from his Parliamentary session in London, and my girls enjoy the company of people their own age. I should very much like to have your and Bella's company as often as I can."

She spoke very seriously, and Lillian couldn't help but believe in her sincerity.

"You are very kind. I am grateful for you, more than you know."

"Well, you are doing me a service, I assure you, in breaking up the tiresomeness of my country life. I can only abide London for short periods, and my son likes a lot of solitude, for studying and reading and the like."

She was finally realizing who the lady meant by "Nash." He was the young Lord Barrentine, her son. Lillian had rarely, if ever, heard the man's Christian name spoken.

Her hostess steered the conversation toward light topics, which was actually quite refreshing after living with her brother and sister-in-law, and before that, Mrs. Courtney.

Soon enough, they were walking out into the garden behind the house and toward the cottage.

"I hope it is satisfactory. The servants have been cleaning it, as it has been empty since my husband's mother lived there, and she passed away more than fifteen years ago. Come, let us go inside."

The cottage was everything she could have hoped for. Of course, it was small compared to Stokemont Abbey or her home where she grew up, but it was quite sufficient for just herself and Bella. It was also much better maintained than the cottage her grandfather had left her on the Isle of Wight.

"It is wonderful, truly," Lillian said. "I love the cozy rooms. There is nothing to keep us from being perfectly happy here."

Bella squirmed to get down. Lillian placed her feet on the floor and she went to the window in the bedroom where Lillian had already decided they would sleep. "Mamma, look at the garden."

"It is a little flower garden we made of all of Lady Barrentine's—my husband's mother's—favorite flowers. She was able to sit in her little chair by the window every day and see her flowers."

"It is beautiful." Blooms of every color in the rainbow waved their colorful petals in the breeze, nodding as if in time to music.

As she considered how God had given her just what she needed, tears sprang to her eyes. How good God was to give her friends from perfect strangers, and to provide a place for her and Bella.

CHAPTER SEVEN

"You received a letter."

Lady Barrentine stood with smiling face at her door, holding out a letter.

"Good morning, and thank you, but you shouldn't trouble yourself."

"Pish-posh. It is no trouble at all."

Lillian invited her inside and they drank a cup of tea, while Bella climbed into Lady Barrentine's lap and played with her hand, comparing her own tiny fingers and hand to the lady's.

"How I've missed this," she said softly, obviously enjoying Bella's attention. When Bella scrambled down from her lap to go fetch her doll, Lady Barrentine said, "I hope to have some grandchildren soon, before I'm too old to enjoy them. But in the meantime, I am very much enjoying your and Bella's company. Truly, I am so glad you have come to stay. I hadn't realized how dull and lifeless this place was. Nash is always doing his studying, which would not bother me if only he would talk to me about it. But he thinks I wouldn't understand, or at least wouldn't enjoy what interests him, or so he tells me."

"You cannot know how grateful I am to be here," Lillian said. Of course, she had cried herself to sleep once or twice, but that was only because she was remembering how badly her husband had treated her, how alone she now was, and wondering if she would ever be loved. A poor widow, with someone else's child? It seemed unlikely any man would ever love her the way she'd dreamed of being loved.

Lillian was careful not to mention Nash, as his mother called him. She did not want any awkwardness or suspicion, on anyone's part, that she might have designs on the young earl. So she made no reply to the lady's remarks about her son.

"You are still quite young," Lillian said. "I am sure you will have plenty of years to enjoy grandchildren."

"I have four children. I should hope that at least one of them will have a child soon. But only one of my daughters is married, and she seems to be enjoying the various entertainments in London too much to think of having children."

"They will come whether she wants them to or not, I daresay."

"You are right about that, my dear."

They both smiled knowingly.

After talking for a while and finishing their tea, Lady Barrentine invited Lillian to dine with her in the evening. "And bring Bella with you."

"You are very kind, but I cannot be dining with you every evening. Not only is there the expense—"

"Say nothing of the expense. Pish, that is nothing."

"There is also the matter of your son, who surely does not enjoy the company of a stranger and her small child every evening at dinner. You both shall tire of me and I shall feel mortified."

"My dear, no one is tiring of you. Nash and I both need the company. And if he doesn't like it, he can go stay at his hunting lodge, or at his townhouse in London."

"Now, that is not fair. He would surely not wish to be so treated—forced from his home because of unwanted guests."

"You are not unwanted, and he spends far too much time in solitude. He will not go to his hunting lodge or to London just because a lovely young woman and her sweet, adorable child occasionally come to dinner."

"Occasionally? It has been every night since I arrived."

"Well, consider it an indulgence of mine. At my age, I deserve some indulgences, I daresay." Lady Barrentine's expression was smug and a little amused, as though she was laughing at herself.

How different she was from Mrs. Courtney.

When Lady Barrentine had gone, Lillian remembered her letter. It was from Mrs. Courtney.

My Dear Lillian and Isabella,

I received your letter informing me that you are planning to stay at Dunbridge Hall in their cottage on the estate. What have I done that you would so mistreat me? That you would take my only granddaughter from me? You say that I can come and visit at any time, but that is absurd, and you know it.

What is the Earl of Barrentine to you? Are you lovers? Is that why you have gone there? What are you exposing my granddaughter to? I do not understand you, but I am not relinquishing my Isabella. I realize you must despise me, but you must think of Isabella, with no servants to wait on her, living in a cottage on the charity of your lover.

Let me be plain. If you do not return Isabella to Stokemont Abbey to be with her own people and to be brought up with the privileges and education she deserves, then I shall be forced to take action through the law. I shall have you investigated for murdering your husband on the Isle of Wight, since his death was very suspicious, and I shall have you declared an incompetent mother. But if you bring Isabella to me, no more shall be said on the subject. Otherwise, you shall be hearing from my solicitor.

Yours,

Mrs. Edward Henshawe Courtney

Lillian's cheeks were burning by the time she finished reading the letter. How dare she accuse her outright of both the murder of her husband and of being a kept woman? Such vile, baseless accusations. But her stomach twisted in knots at her mother-in-law's threat of taking Bella from her. She had no money for hiring someone to defend her in court, and Mrs. Courtney would certainly hire the best solicitor and barrister that money could buy.

"God, please save us," she whispered.

~ ~ ~

Nash was deep in thought, mulling over his new story and its characters, when he saw Lillian and her young daughter walking hand-in-hand in the garden beyond his window. The realization came over him, not for the first time, that the heroine he was writing about was actually Lillian Courtney.

How had this happened?

He'd come up with the story idea after saving her

from her assailant in the village of Gantt. That incident had certainly taken hold of his imagination, but it was rather disturbing that he had so romanticized, even in his mind, but especially on paper, the plight of a young widow and her child. And his mother was determined to have her in their home every night for dinner.

Truthfully, he didn't mind. He enjoyed her company and even enjoyed the endearing antics of her little Bella. But that was the most disturbing part. He shouldn't enjoy their company so much. It was annoying. And dangerous.

If his identity as the author Perceval Hastings were discovered, then if he started writing about a young widow and an earl who saves her, people would naturally assume that Mrs. Lillian Courtney was more to him than simply a friend of his mother's, or a tenant, or someone they were helping out of kindness, as she actually was. Of course, Nash was relying on no one discovering his identity any time soon, but he never knew when it might happen.

He had been trying to make the pretty young widow in his story to be something of a villain, but it simply was not working out. The more he tried to make the Italian count or the English earl her victim, the more blocked he became, sitting at his desk for minutes that stretched into hours, unable to write the next line.

In defeat, he had gone back to writing her as the innocent one and settled for changing the English earl into a clergyman to try and make it seem less identical to his own situation.

He was also having trouble figuring out what the Italian count's role was as villain. But for that he tried to draw inspiration from the very novels he was satirizing.

After all, their villains were often ridiculous, their motives random and indistinct.

Of course. His count could be obsessed with the young widow, for no particular reason that anyone could see, and he could have fun with that for several pages.

But something else was starting to bother him. What was the actual purpose of his satirical novels? Did he truly want to be remembered as someone who ridiculed others? After all, one literary critic had said his books were "the perfect foil for today's popular novels." Did he want to be someone else's foil?

One comment had stuck in his head that a fellow author, he couldn't remember who, had once said: It is easy to criticize but difficult to create. And Nash's novels were basically a criticism.

What would happen if he created a story that was unique and completely his own? Something that represented his own thoughts and beliefs, but was written to entertain and delight the reader?

He had to ponder this some more. His publisher, after all, was paying him to write satires. In fact, his editor would sometimes break into donkey-braying laughter when telling Nash his favorite part of his novel. Nash was happy he could make people laugh, but if it was at the expense of another author . . .

He was obviously losing his taste for satire.

He tried to concentrate and write the next line in his story, but his eyes kept drifting back to Lillian and Bella outside in the garden. As he watched them, he began to think that Lillian seemed troubled. He wasn't sure if it was the tilt of her shoulders, the way she moved, or something else, as he couldn't even see the expression on her face, as it was turned away from him.

Perhaps he was going daft. But he hoped she would be at dinner tonight so that his mother could discover the reason, if indeed something was wrong.

~ ~ ~

After dinner, they were in the drawing room. Bella had fallen asleep on the sofa beside Lillian.

"My dear, is something troubling you?" Mother asked.

Nash let out a pent-up breath, glad his mother had finally asked the question he had wanted to ask all day.

Lillian hesitated, then said, "Forgive me. I do not wish to burden you with my troubles."

"We will not consider anything you say to be a burden. Please, share with us what is on your mind."

She sighed, a look of conflicting emotions on her face. "I received a letter from my mother-in-law, Mrs. Courtney, today."

"Oh yes, the letter I brought to you. Was it bad news?"

"Yes. It seems Mrs. Courtney is very angry with me for bringing Bella here to live. She is demanding that I bring my child to live at Stokemont Abbey."

"But she is inviting you to live there too, is she not?" Mother asked.

"No. In fact . . ." Lillian sighed, then took a deep breath as her chin started to quiver.

Nash's chest ached to see her so upset. He waited for her to go on, but inside he was seething at that cold-hearted Mrs. Courtney.

After a few moments, and with obvious effort, she continued. "Forgive me, but Mrs. Courtney is making wild accusations against me. She says if I don't bring Bella to live with her, she will have me investigated for murdering my husband—which I did not do, of course. I had nothing to do with it. I—"

"My dear, you do not have to say any more about that. I would never believe it of you."

Nash was thinking that if she had murdered him, he probably deserved it. Nash knew the man to be rash, ill-tempered, and even prone to picking fights, but always with men who were physically smaller than he was.

"She says she will have me declared an incompetent mother and take my child away from me, and I fear that she will be able to do it; I have not the means to hire a barrister to try to stop her." Her voice was shaky, and she had one hand on Bella's back, her other hand clenched and half hidden in her skirt.

"Oh, my," Mother said, catching her breath. "That is despicable."

Indeed.

Nash tried to think how he could help the young widow to keep her child. But how could he help her and yet prevent his interference from becoming known? No doubt Mrs. Courtney—and most other people as well—would think she was more to him than just a tenant, and the scandal would ruin both their reputations.

But his silence might make her think he was not sympathetic, so he said, "Mrs. Courtney would be cruel and heartless indeed if she follows through with these threats."

"I am not trying to keep Bella from her," Lillian said in a quiet voice, no doubt very aware that her daughter was asleep beside her and not wishing to wake her. "But I do have concerns about her, seeing the way she has taken charge of her other grandchild, a little boy two years older than Bella. I fear that she will . . ."

"Will what, my dear?" Mother was leaning toward her.

"Forgive me, but . . . her son was not a very good father or husband, and I fear that the way his mother brought him up, certain things she says and does . . . I fear that she will turn her grandchildren into just the sort of people her son was, if she is allowed to take charge of them. Perhaps that is foolish."

"Not foolish at all," Mother said. "A parent is the child's greatest influence, even with nurses and other servants caring for the child. 'Evil companions corrupt good morals,' but if the parent doesn't instill good morals in the first place, or in some way distorts the child's sense of what is true, it can be quite detrimental to the child's temperament."

"Most importantly, she is your child," Nash interjected. "Her grandmother shouldn't be allowed to speak lies about you in order to take the child from her mother."

"Yes, my dear. We will not allow it. We shall let Mrs. Courtney know that you are not without friends, and perhaps she will not follow through on her threats."

"You are so very kind, and you have done so much for me already. I cannot bear to see you get involved in such a sordid affair, with the kind of accusations that Mrs. Courtney is making. At the same time, I cannot bear to lose my daughter."

Lillian's voice broke on her last word and tears fell from her eyes. She quickly bent her head and wiped at her tears with a handkerchief that was clutched in her hand.

"Oh, my dear." Mother's expression was pained, and she moved closer so she could squeeze the young woman's arm.

Nash was shocked at how her obvious distress

affected him. His face warmed and he could feel his blood pounding in his temples, as if he was ready to physically defend this poor woman and attack her enemies.

His reaction was quite similar to the characters in the novels he satirized.

How demoralizing.

If he were thinking rationally, he would remind himself of how his involvement in this woman's troubles could indeed cause him years of trouble. What if this Mrs. Courtney turned her accusations on him? Perhaps it would even endanger his chances of marrying the kind of young woman he hoped to eventually engage—someone without reproach, innocent and good, and from a proper family.

Rational thinking sounded cowardly.

"Forgive me for being so selfish," Lillian said. "You have already done so much to help me. I do not deserve your kindness." She seemed to have calmed herself.

He couldn't help thinking that she was incredibly pretty, especially when he considered how ugly his sisters looked when they cried.

"You are not being selfish," Mother said, with a tone of gentle scolding. "You are allowing us to know your troubles. And if we are able and willing to help you, then that is not your responsibility, it is ours."

His mother was obviously including him in the helping.

"Let us hope that Mrs. Courtney will not follow through on her threats," Mother said, "that she will think better of it, or that her threats were only meant to manipulate you and that she had no intention of carrying them out."

Lillian nodded, but he did not think his mother's

words were very reassuring for her.

"I should go, but I thank you for the invitation to dinner and for all your many kindnesses."

"I shall find a servant to carry little Bella for you," Mother said.

"No, no, I shall manage very well. I am used to carrying her." Lillian lifted the child and placed her on her shoulder. The child barely stirred and continued to sleep.

Mother and two servants carrying lanterns walked Lillian to the cottage, and when Mother returned, Nash was still in the drawing room. Mother came near and whispered, "Her husband hit her, twice, and that is why she left and went to the Isle of Wight."

"She told you this?"

"Yes."

Nash's hands clenched into fists. Never before had he wished to kill anyone, but he actually wished he could strike the man in his ugly face. Unfortunately, he was already dead.

"When I asked her if he had struck her, she said he had, on two different occasions."

"Truly, what sort of man hits a woman?"

"I suspected he had done so because of the way she hangs her head—it reminds me of your Aunt Roberta."

His mother's sister had married a man who turned out to be a most unfortunate choice for a husband. He beat his wife quite often, until one winter night after getting so drunk he fell asleep in a ditch and froze to death.

Lillian Courtney did not remind him of his aunt, but it was true that sometimes she did seem to possess a certain humility that was quite a contrast to the pride and arrogance of most women of her social status.

Being struck by someone who was supposed to

love, honor, and protect you would certainly cause feelings of humiliation, he imagined. His blood fairly boiled just thinking about it.

He prayed later that night when he was alone in his room, "God, if you wish to use me to help Lillian Courtney and her child, then I will not be a coward. I will do what you need to me to do."

But if God did want to use him, how would he know? Perhaps God wanted him to use wisdom and discretion. Truthfully, if he was able to help the woman, he would not be able to refrain from doing so, as his emotions, he was certain, would demand his action.

CHAPTER EIGHT

In spite of the gratitude that washed over her at Lady and Lord Barrentine's concern and promises of help, Lillian cried herself to sleep that night, but quietly, so as not to awaken Bella.

To have married into *such* a family! Lillian alternated between disgust at herself, and the pain of knowing that God could have stopped her somehow but had chosen not to.

Her poor child would grow up without a father, and now, possibly, without her mother.

Lillian could not indulge that thought for long. It was too painful, an actual pain inside her chest that made her wonder if there was something ailing her.

She awoke praying, "God, please don't take my child from me." She opened her eyes to see Bella sit up and rub her eyes.

Perhaps she should spend the day praying, as she'd once heard a homily on praying over important situations and decisions, but her nerves would not allow her to put off replying to Mrs. Courtney's letter.

Before the morning was over, she was sitting down to write it.

> *My Dear Mother-In-Law, Mrs. Courtney,*
> *I was very surprised to receive your letter and to find such horrifying accusations and threats.*

No. That sounded too hostile and defensive. Lillian started again.

> *My Dear Mrs. Courtney,*
> *Your last letter gave me great sorrow. I have no intention of keeping your granddaughter from you and I can bring her to Stokemont Abbey for frequent visits. I love her more than anyone in the world and will give her all the motherly love that she deserves. I have no wish to have any enmity between us. Please know that I will love Bella and will not allow her to suffer want. Please write back and let me know when you would like to have a visit from Bella and I shall bring her.*
> *Yours Respectfully,*
> *Lillian Courtney*

It was short and made no direct mention of Mrs. Courtney's threats and accusations. Perhaps it would soothe the woman's ruffled feathers, even though it was not what her mother-in-law wanted, which was total compliance and a surrendering of Bella into her hands. But that was something Lillian would never do. Surely Mrs. Courtney would understand that and be satisfied.

~ ~ ~

Two days later, Lillian saw Lady Barrentine hurrying across the garden toward her cottage and went out to meet her. In her hand was what looked like a letter.

Lillian's heart beat so hard and fast, it made her stomach sick.

"Is it another letter from Mrs. Courtney?" Lillian asked before Lady Barrentine even reached her.

"It is. I knew you would want to read it at once. Shall I go and let you read it in private?"

"No, please stay. Bella is taking her nap, so I will read it before she awakens."

Lillian opened the letter and read it quickly, then aloud for Lady Barrentine.

"Since you insist upon defying me, and since I take your silence to be an admission of guilt, I have turned this matter over to my solicitors and barristers in London. They shall take the proper action against you for what you have done."

Lady Barrentine looked aghast. "Did she write anything else?"

"No." Lillian showed her the letter so she could see how short it was. Would she be sent to prison? Would Bella be taken from her forever and sent to live with Mrs. Courtney? Her hands were shaking and she could barely breathe.

"The very great nerve of that woman," Lady Barrentine said. "And what does she mean, they shall take action against you for what you have done?"

Lillian retrieved Mrs. Courtney's previous letter and gave it to Lady Barrentine to read.

"The nerve! The utter cheek! The woman has lost her senses to make such unfounded accusations."

"But what must I do? What can I do? I cannot bear to lose Bella, but I don't know how to fight her. I'm terrified." She was aware that she was speaking her thoughts aloud in a strangled whisper, but she couldn't seem to stop. "I have no money, no family. My brother has his own troubles, but I suppose I can go to him and beg for help." She could feel the blood draining from her face.

"My dear, you do not look well. Come and sit down here." Lady Barrentine led her to a sofa and they both sat. "Now, listen to me. You are not without friends. Indeed, we shall fight any such thing that Mrs. Courtney tries to do. The nerve of that woman, to accuse you and my son of wrongdoing, simply because you are living in our cottage. Well, do not worry, my dear. We have our own solicitors and barristers, and they are the best in England. We shall come to your aid."

Lillian put her head in her hands. It was her worst nightmare come true, and she was too horrified to cry. "You must not endanger yourselves. Indeed, you mustn't. Lord Barrentine is young and does not deserve to have his name defiled. I cannot allow you to help me any longer. I must go. Bella and I shall go—"

"Where would you go?"

"I will go and stay with my brother."

"You were very unhappy there. You told me so yourself."

"It matters not about my happiness. I cannot lose Bella. No, we shall all be safer if I go."

"There, there, you must be calm." Lady Barrentine laid a gentle hand on her forearm. "We shall both be calm and take deep breaths, like this." She took in a slow, long breath, then let it out slowly.

Lillian tried to comply, but it was impossible, as tight as her chest was. The air simply would not go in. *O God, help me! Don't take Bella from me.*

Lady Barrentine sat beside her, a quiet, calm presence, while Lillian concentrated on simply breathing.

"Good girl." Lady Barrentine's voice was comforting, even though Lillian still felt as if her chest was too tight to allow the proper amount of air.

Bella's whimpering sounds, which she often made when she was waking up from a nap, came from the bedroom.

"I'll go get her," Lillian said, jumping up and hurrying to her daughter.

She was a mother, and she could not frighten or upset Bella, could not think of losing her, or she would start sobbing.

I will not think of it. I cannot. I must believe that all will be well.

"There's my sweet girl," she said cheerfully but softly, lifting her three-year-old into her arms and holding her close. "All is well. Did you wake up from your nap? Come, and I shall get you some water, and you shall see Lady Barrentine. Would you like that?"

Bella made an indistinct answer that was nonetheless understood as a yes as she wrapped her small hands around her mother's neck, her doll tucked under her arm.

They talked softly, about the flowers that were blooming in the garden and in the hedges, about the weather and how pleasant it had been, until Bella began to be more awake and alert.

"I shall leave you now," Lady Barrentine said, "and I will write to the appropriate people. Nothing has happened as yet, so we shall put away all worry. It is only threats and unfounded accusations, which may all come to nothing. So I shan't have you worrying. Leave it to me, and I shall expect you both to dine with us tonight. Bella, will you bring your Mamma to dinner tonight?"

Bella nodded, her eyes wide.

"Good. I shall expect you early, and no worrying in the meantime."

Lillian nodded and watched her walk toward the main house, knowing it would be a very long afternoon, trying not to worry, trying to cast her care on the Lord. She also prayed silently for wisdom.

Was she desperate enough—or selfish enough—to allow Lord Barrentine's mother to help her, possibly sacrificing his reputation in the process?

God, forgive me. Help me.

~ ~ ~

Nash reread the letter his friend had sent from London.

The third person has just asked me if I knew you were the novelist Perceval Hastings. Apparently, it was printed in the Examiner *yesterday, along with an excerpt from the newest manuscript that hasn't been published yet. Is it true? You will surely laugh at me for even asking. You should sue the* Examiner *for libel.*

No one had access to his newest manuscript except his publisher. Had his publisher purposely revealed his identity in the hopes of selling more books?

Nash ran his hand over his face and blew out a breath. He was sure to receive a lot of abuse from his sisters, not to mention his fellow Members of Parliament. But he had known all along that this might happen. He'd only hoped it wouldn't happen so soon.

This, on the heels of his mother explaining to him that Mrs. Courtney was accusing Lillian of murdering her husband and being Nash's paramour, while the woman used her solicitors to take Bella away from her.

"I know if we get involved it may harm your reputation, but your reputation is so untouched, so sterling, I can't imagine that this one little thing could make a difference. And I'd like to see if our barristers can help her. If you are worried about it, however, I shall try to keep our name as quiet as possible, but you know how impossible that is."

He had two choices, and one was the coward's way.

"I am happy to help, even if it sacrifices my reputation." Mother did not know it yet, but his reputation was not so sterling anymore.

Mother had frowned, looked sad and worried, but Nash reassured her, "I'm not concerned what gossips say, Mother. After all, I'm not one to try to move in the highest social circles. You know I don't care about that. And when I'm ready to marry, I certainly don't want to marry someone who cares about lies and false accusations, so it's of no consequence what people say about me and Lillian Courtney."

Indeed, Mother was so determined to help Lillian, so outraged that Mrs. Courtney would try to take Bella from her, that she seemed cheered by his assertions and went straight to her writing desk to pen some letters to their solicitors and barristers in London.

His reputation was as good as in tatters. The next time he walked into Parliament, his fellow members might very well laugh him to scorn. It would be worse if they should look at him askance and whisper behind his back.

But he would be above caring about such things.

At least it would be for a noble cause if he garnered scorn and false accusations because of helping Lillian. Losing his reputation simply because he enjoyed writing and publishing his novels seemed infinitely less noble.

And yet, he was proud of his work—although the thought of strangers reading his thoughts and knowing he had written them made some heat creep into his face. But he had nothing to be ashamed of.

Truly, it was his family he worried about the most. What would Mother and his sisters say? Would they be disappointed in him, as his father had been? How would it affect them?

When he thought of all that Lillian was going through, the threat of having her daughter taken from her, accused of a crime she never committed, he realized his own troubles were small in comparison. And he hated to think of sweet little Bella having to endure a life in Mrs. Courtney's control, taken from her mother, never to see her again.

And what of the villain who tried to harm Lillian in the village of Gantt? Could there have been something more behind his actions than just a random robbery? He'd never heard from the constable about whether or not the man had been located, and the authorities may not have contacted Lillian either, as she had left the county. And of course, if Mrs. Courtney had heard anything, she would not be a good source of information.

Nash would go to the little village and search out the constable, first thing in the morning.

With any luck, he might be away from home when his mother and sisters discovered that he was publishing satirical novels under a false name.

CHAPTER NINE

Nash left the carriage at home and rode his horse in a drizzly rain all the way to the village of Gantt.

He found the constable fairly quickly. He was drinking at the village's only alehouse.

After the initial greetings, Nash said, "I don't suppose you found the man in question, the one who assaulted the younger Mrs. Courtney."

The constable's eyes shifted around the room and he rubbed his chin before answering.

"I looked but didn't find him."

"Did you discover his name or anything about him?"

"I didn't."

"I'm surprised Mrs. Courtney, the younger lady's mother-in-law, did not make it worth your while to keep searching."

The constable used his hand to cup his chin and shift his jaw with an audible popping sound, as if popping it back in place. Then he said, "Well, now, as a matter of fact, she told me not to bother with searching for the man."

"Did she give a reason?"

"If I recollect, she just said Mrs. Courtney—the younger one—was well and was not in any danger."

And how would she know that?

"I see. Well, I would like to request that you continue to search for the man who accosted the younger Mrs. Courtney. The lady would like to have him found and brought to justice."

"She would? Well, I cannot very well go against Mrs. Courtney's wishes—the elder Mrs. Courtney, I mean—seeing as she resides here in the village and the younger Mrs. Courtney does not. You can see what a bad position that puts me in, this being my only jurisdiction."

Nash said nothing.

"But, now, if you, my lord, would make it worth my while, I could go back to searching."

The constable was asking for a bribe! Nash had never encountered such a thing before. Well, it was worth it. And thankfully, he happened to have two five-pound notes in his pocket. He pulled them out, quickly folded and handed them to the constable, whose own hand was ready to receive them.

The man glanced down at the notes, probably in order to see what they were. He must have been pleased with the amount because he winked and said, "I shall keep looking for the man."

"Send me word as soon as you find him, and if you apprehend him and hold him until I arrive, I shall give you three times that amount."

"Yes, my lord." The constable licked his lips, then bowed.

Nash left the alehouse and the village, but then circled back and glanced around the streets, just in case, but he did not see Lillian's assailant. He rode home, arriving so late that he missed dinner. Strangely, he found himself feeling a lowering in his spirits at having missed seeing Lillian and Bella.

~ ~ ~

"Please don't trouble yourself, my dear," Lady Barrentine had said at dinner after Lillian begged her not to endanger her or her son's reputation on her behalf.

Lady Barrentine was obviously trying to keep her son out of the fray, and for that Lillian was glad.

Nash, as his mother called him, did not even dine with them. Lillian did not ask where he had gone, of course, and his mother offered no explanation. No doubt he was gone to London to be seen there in order to keep the gossips from saying that he was with Lillian.

But the next morning she saw him striding toward the stables.

So he hadn't gone to London. She said a silent prayer for God to protect his reputation, even as she thanked God for Lady Barrentine's help. She was shameless for letting that good woman help her, but she just couldn't bear to lose Bella or to see her under Mrs. Courtney's control—being smothered and praised higher than the angels one minute, and criticized and shamed the next.

A few days later, an official-looking letter came for her. Lady Barrentine stayed with her while she opened and read it.

By the time she finished it, her hands were shaking and she handed it to Lady Barrentine.

"This is from the office of a well-known barrister." The lady perused the letter and her expression grew more sober until she finally lowered the letter and raised her head to look at Lillian. "Don't listen to a word he says. He cannot take your child away. He is no judge and has no authority. He's only a bully, trying to intimidate you into handing Bella over to her grandmother, which you will not do. Do not listen to his bluster. Only a judge has the authority to . . . I shall, with your permission, copy this letter and send it to my barrister in London. I have no doubt that he can pen a letter just as bullying. These barristers are paid to lie and threaten and accuse. Pay it no mind, my dear."

But how could she pay it no mind? The man was indeed threatening and accusing, and with every word he sent fear straight to Lillian's heart like a spear that cut through and lodged there. Her knees went weak again, as they had when she first read the letter. Her strength was leaving her, the blood draining from her face.

"Lillian, listen to me." Lady Barrentine took hold of her arm and stared into her eyes. "Be brave, now. Do not lose heart. I can see you are frightened by this letter, but do not heed it. Promise me you will not believe a word he is saying. He cannot take your child away on Mrs. Courtney's behalf without the authority of the Court of Chancery. And such a thing would take time and some kind of evidence to support his claims."

"He claims that they are preparing to have me committed to an insane asylum."

"I will not let that happen, so do not heed it. Do you trust me?"

Lillian nodded. But the letter had her heart pumping so hard it gave her a headache. How could anyone write such a cruel, threatening letter—anyone besides Mrs. Courtney?

"I can't understand how that man could say such things to me. He doesn't even know me."

"That is the way of barristers. They say such things because they consider it their job, almost their duty to the person on whose behalf they are speaking. It's just a game, and it's how the game is played, so do not let it upset you. Now, you shall dine with me tonight and we shall not worry at all. My daughter Mildred shall be home tonight and she will play and sing for us and make us both quite merry, I daresay. Leave this all to me. I shall write to my own barrister, and I daresay he will be able to bully and intimidate the opposing side as well as you ever might hope."

Indeed, Lady Barrentine looked quite confident and unworried. And she took the offensive letter with her, which was just as well, as Lillian never wanted to read it again.

~ ~ ~

Miss Mildred Golding was pleasant enough, and she did indeed play and sing for them, even before dinner was served. But Nash seemed quieter and more sober than usual, and he and his sister spoke not a word to each other until they were served the final course.

"I suppose we are not talking of Nash's folly and how it is being reported in the papers," Mildred suddenly announced, "but I'm sure Lillian has heard the news by now, even out here in the country."

Nash glared at her, a look Lillian had never seen on his face before.

"Let us not spoil dinner with gossip," Lady Barrentine said quietly.

"It isn't gossip, Mother. My brother is a published novelist, and we had to hear it from the newspapers. No matter that it only gives the jealous people of the world the fodder and license to laugh at us. No matter that respectable men will stay away from my sister and me."

"Don't be so dramatic," Lady Barrentine said, looking as if she was trying to smile and make light of the situation, while Nash rolled his eyes to the ceiling and glared.

Lillian wanted to ask what they were speaking of, but she said nothing, feeling the awkwardness and tension in the room.

Mildred looked at Lillian and said, "Forgive me. I am being rude. It seems that my brother, Nash Golding, Fourth Earl of Barrentine, is actually writing and publishing satirical novels under the name Perceval Hastings. Can you imagine? A Member of the House of Lords, and he's spending his time writing satires, ridiculing some of the most popular novelists of our time, and earning money for them."

"Mildred, this is not the time or place," Lady Barrentine said.

No one else spoke for several moments, then Nash said, "In my defense . . . I've made very little money."

Mildred looked angry as she glared down at her plate, set her fork down noisily, and shot a deadly look at her brother. "Everyone is laughing at us. There are cartoon drawings of you in the newspapers. What was your purpose in this, pray tell?"

"Why, to annoy you, sister dear." Nash looked and sounded as unconcerned as if they were speaking of a fly that was disturbing his sister's peace.

"Actions have consequences," Mildred said.

"If you think I care about social standing and what the vain gossipmongers of high society think of me, you are mistaken."

"You may not care, but you have endangered my chances of marrying well, and Emma's chances. Do you not understand that?"

"Mildred, please," Lady Barrentine said in a hushed but insistent voice. "This is hardly good dinner conversation. And Lillian cannot possibly wish to hear of such tidings. She has much worse troubles of her own."

Everyone was silent while Lillian took in this information.

So, Nash was writing novels, satires in fact, under an assumed name. Why should that be such a terrible thing? But she knew how society was. They thought gentlemen, and especially titled gentlemen, should do nothing to earn money, nothing that smacked of work. Indeed, she was rather surprised that he would publish his novels. After all, something scientific or academic might have been accepted, especially if he donated all monies earned to a scientific society for the exploration of an uncharted country, or the preservation of a rare beetle. But a novel, and especially a satirical one? This was something that the caricaturists could sink their teeth into. Certainly, it should sell lots of newspapers.

But poor Nash. She was sorry for him, for she knew him to be a quiet sort who did not enjoy attention or notoriety. He was no Lord Byron, and indeed, was that poet's opposite in behavior and morality, if Lillian understood them both correctly. And he couldn't be enjoying his sister's angry censure.

Nash and his sister both looked as if they had nothing more to say, having been chastised by their mother.

"Forgive us for our inconsiderate and contentious talk," Nash said quietly, directing his speech to Lillian. "It was most impolite."

Mildred said, "Yes, do forgive us," but with a shuttered expression.

"There is nothing to forgive," Lillian said. "I had not heard anything of the sort, but I am sorry for anything cruel that has been said to or about anyone in this family, which has been so kind to me. And I must say, I should very much like to read Lord Barrentine's novels. I am sure they would make me forget my own troubles, especially if they have a lot of ghosts, haunted houses, and frightening kidnappers who turn out to be nothing more than lonely and matrimonial."

Mildred's smile was almost reluctant, while Nash's face broke into an amused half grin.

"It does sound as if Lillian might enjoy your novels, Nash," his mother said. "Please do give her a copy of each of them. She needs something diverting."

They began to talk of their favorite novels and to ask Nash to explain the plots of his novels. He complied. As it turned out, he'd just sent his third novel to the publisher.

"I started the first one when I was eighteen. Life at school was dull, and I did not like drinking or playing at cards, so I read and wrote my own stories to pass the time. After reading a few of the popular, overly dramatic novels, which were full of overwrought situations with victimized heroines in distress and villainous guardians in decrepit old castles, it was too easy to poke fun at them. I suppose I wanted to hear what other people thought of my novel, when I was finished, but I wasn't bold enough to show it to anyone who knew me, so I sent it to a publisher. I was surprised when he accepted it for publication. And since I thought I could keep my identity as the author a secret, as many authors endeavor to do these days, I allowed them to publish it."

Mildred shook her head, frowning.

Lady Barrentine smiled and said, "I am very proud of my son, the published novelist."

Mildred made a slight sound indicating disgust.

"I think it was very brave." Lillian hadn't meant to voice her thoughts. Or at any rate, she regretted them afterward, as everyone turned to look at her. She felt her cheeks starting to turn red.

The expression on Nash's face as he looked at her was one of surprise and—dare she call it tenderness? Her stomach did an unladylike flip. Indeed, she couldn't remember her husband ever giving her such a tender look —kind and grateful at the same time. But there was even more to the look, as if he was reading her thoughts while knowing she was reading his.

Surely such a thing was absurd. She was letting her imagination run wild, the result of too many tense and traumatic events in one week.

"Do you play, Mrs. Courtney?" Mildred asked, then, before Lillian could answer, she suggested they retire to the drawing room.

"Only a little," Lillian replied.

"I haven't asked her to play," Lady Barrentine said, "as she has endured so many harrowing events of late."

"And usually I have my daughter with me," Lillian explained. "She falls asleep as soon as we go to the drawing room."

Mildred looked slightly aghast. "You bring your daughter to dine? Is she not three years old?"

"She is."

"Bella is the sweetest child, Mildred," Lady Barrentine said. "You will adore her, and she is no trouble, very quiet."

"She would be welcome to dine here even if she were noisy and danced on top of the table," Nash said in a very matter-of-fact voice.

Lillian's breath went right out of her chest at his words, while Lady Barrentine stifled a laugh. Mildred stared, open-mouthed, at her brother, then closed her mouth as a look of disgust marred her pretty features.

"Little Bella is sleeping in my room at the moment," Lady Barrentine explained, "and Helen is watching her while she does the mending."

Lillian did not like leaving her daughter in anyone else's care, especially someone she was unfamiliar with, but Helen had been with Lady Barrentine's household since Nash was born, and she was an older woman with white hair and a kindly smile.

"Why don't you sing for us, Mildred, dear?" Lady Barrentine seated herself beside Lillian and Mildred took her place at the beautiful instrument at the other end of the room. She leafed through the sheets of music, chose one, and started to play. When she finished that song, she chose another and accompanied herself.

Her voice was lovely, and Lillian closed her eyes to listen, trying not to think about the letter she'd received, the ugly threats and accusations it contained, or the fact that Lady Barrentine's daughter did not seem to approve of Nash. And if she did not approve of her brother, she certainly wouldn't approve of Lillian living there in the dowager cottage.

No doubt she considered Lillian and Bella's presence to be a threat to the whole family's reputation—and she would be right. And the guilt of possibly bringing harm to those who had become so dear to her and had been so kind was a sickening weight on her shoulders—adding to all the others.

CHAPTER TEN

Nash awoke early the next morning with the same thoughts on his mind that had plagued him before he fell asleep. He got dressed and readied himself to go for a long ride while he thought things over.

He'd always known his sister was arrogant, but he'd never thought of her as unkind—until now. But Mildred was prideful, and there was no other way to think of it. Mother would never accuse her of such a thing, but Nash would not deny what he was clearly seeing in her.

Truthfully, he had no wish to harm his sisters' reputations. As a man, his own reputation could be restored quite easily, and a bad reputation was not so injurious to him, causing him little more than a bit of ribbing from his peers. But it was a much more serious matter for his sisters because they were female, their place in society being so much more precarious. It was an unfair truth, but a truth nevertheless. So perhaps he should not judge Mildred so harshly.

Still, he did not appreciate his sister taking the view that most people seemed to take—that small children were inferior to adults in every way and should be kept quiet and hidden away, unworthy of being seen or heard. But Nash had memories from when he was hardly older than Bella, and he knew that small children were capable of feeling and understanding a great many things.

So, as unusual as it was for Lillian Courtney to care for her own child and take her with her everywhere she went, he also found it refreshing. He saw empathy in Lillian, which was especially obvious in how she interacted with her daughter, as well as with Nash's mother. It was an empathy that touched Nash's heart, if he was honest.

Nash's experience with women was negligent at best. He'd had the one incident with Henrietta Caldwell, which was harrowing and left him even more cautious than he was by nature, and if he were to become enamored with Lillian simply because she was in close proximity—the first unmarried, unrelated woman to be so—then what kind of fool would he appear to be? And yet he did not think any man who married Lillian Courtney would be considered a fool. No, Nash would consider him blessed and highly favored.

As he rode his horse down the narrow country lane, it was early and no one was about, but he would probably look a bit deranged, shaking his head and muttering under his breath as he was. But he kept going. He needed to sort this out.

Certainly, a man could do worse than Lillian, with her kind nature, obvious good moral character, and lovely face and figure, but he knew what his sisters would say: "She has no fortune, her family is neither old nor distinguished, and she is a widow with a child." Even his mother, who was greatly attached to both Lillian and her daughter, might disapprove. After all, she was forever saying, "Much is expected of the Earl of Barrentine, and much will be expected of his wife."

But there was a higher power than society, One who should be of greater influence even than his family; Providence should be his highest authority.

But he could not simply ask God a question and wait for him to answer it, or find a prophet who could cast lots to hear directly from Him, as men in the Bible often did.

If only he could.

When he arrived back at the stable, the groom named Merritt met him outside.

"Sir, there was a man lurking about."

Nash dismounted from his horse. "Who was he? Where?"

"Never seen him 'afore. He was standing over by the big sycamore tree, just staring out this way. I hollered at him and asked him what his business was, and he just turned away sullen-like and walked off into the trees."

"Did he have a broken tooth in front?"

"I could not say, sir. I didn't get a look at his teeth."

"But you're sure it was not any of our tenants?"

"No, sir. I believe I know all your tenant farmers, sir, and he was not any of yours."

"Was he tall?"

"No, sir, not particularly. Do you want I should go look for him? He's only been gone a half hour."

"Yes, Merritt, take a horse and set out in search. If you find him, get his name and where he lives, but if you don't find him in half an hour or so, leave off searching."

"Yes, sir." Merritt looked quite intent, taking his assignment seriously.

Nash mounted his horse again and searched the property around the house and the cottage, making sure the man was not still lurking about. After seeing no one, he was on his way back to the stable when he saw Lillian and Bella having a picnic on a blanket among the flowers behind the cottage. He walked toward them.

"Good morning," Lillian said.

"I have a new doll," Bella said, holding up the doll his mother had sent from London. But her old doll was still the favorite, as it was sitting in her lap, while she plunked the new doll down in front of the old one, as if the two were having an intimate conversation.

"Your mother's gift to Bella." Lillian smiled. Even with her troubles, her smile was quite lovely. How much lovelier would she look if she was truly happy and had fewer worries?

He decided not to tell her about the man lurking about. There was no need in alarming her, as the man was probably not the same one who had attacked her in the village.

She looked as if she might say something, then seemed to think better of it. Then he remembered.

"I promised to let you read my first two novels."

"You did indeed." Her smile returned.

"I shall send those over to you today."

Truthfully, he dreaded going home, as he would be sure to be confronted with more newspapers and their stories and caricatures of him and his novels. The very thought made him feel a bit sick. But why should he care what those people said of him? He didn't know them. They had nothing to do with his happiness. But unfortunately, they did make him wish, if only sometimes, that he'd never published his novels.

He bid Lillian and Bella a good day and went back to the stable, just as Merritt was returning.

"Sorry, sir. I didn't see him."

"Very well. Let me know immediately if you do see him again."

"Yes, sir."

"Good man."

Surely the blighter would not come onto his estate to attack Lillian again. But if he was so foolish, Nash would not let him get away this time.

~ ~ ~

The next day, Lillian was enjoying her book— Nash's first book, which he had sent over to her—while Bella played with her dolls and her tea set on the floor.

She was reading the part of the book where the villain was threatening to lock the heroine in the dungeon of the haunted castle, where the ghost of her young cousin walked, moaning and crying. The heroine swooned, fainting dead away, and the villain went to fetch a servant to revive her.

Lillian smiled and shook her head, remembering when her own villain had not only threatened her, but had grabbed her around the throat. Why hadn't she thought to swoon? Perhaps her attacker would have gone to fetch someone to help her. She laughed to herself.

But she knew Nash's intention, as the author, was to show how silly these sorts of novels were, and his story was amusing, but she wondered what he might write if he were serious about telling his own story, a story that was important to him. She suspected she would enjoy *that* story even more.

A knock came at the front door and Lillian went to answer it.

"Oh, Lillian, I am sorry to disturb you. Were you busy?" Lady Barrentine sounded slightly out of breath.

"I was reading Lord Barrentine's novel, *The Mysteries of Greymere Castle*."

"Oh? Well, I have news, my dear, or I would not disturb you."

By her worried look, Lillian guessed it was not good news.

"Can you come to the house and take tea with me? I can have one of the maidservants distract Bella while we talk."

"Of course."

They walked over to the main house. Lillian wondered at her friend coming herself instead of sending a servant to fetch her, but perhaps she was getting her exercise for the day.

Once they were inside the house, Lady Barrentine installed Bella with the cook and a kitchen maid.

"We are making gingerbread cakes, and we need your help," the cook said to Bella.

"You will get the first taste," the kitchen maid said merrily.

"I will be waiting for a cake," Lillian told Bella, who looked as if she took her task seriously.

"We are just in the next room," Lady Barrentine said. "Come and fetch us if you need help with the cakes."

As soon as they were in the room next to the kitchen, which was a sort of work room for the servants and storage room for linens, Lady Barrentine began to speak quickly and quietly.

"Forgive me for ushering you in here—very inhospitable of me—but I didn't want anyone to overhear us, and I shall be brief. I received this letter half an hour ago by special courier." She produced a letter and held it out to Lillian. "It is from my solicitor in London, and I'm afraid it is troubling news, but nothing terribly unexpected. And you should know that I will help you fight this. My solicitor is very competent and has powerful friends, in fact. So do not worry."

But Lady Barrentine's manner sent a pang of fear through her stomach. She took the letter and read it quickly, her heart starting to pound.

Mrs. Edward Courtney's solicitor has sent a brief to Ingleburt Heinz, considered one of the best barristers in England. He is to petition the Court of Chancery on Mrs. Courtney's behalf for guardianship of her son's child, the reasons being that the child's mother is of unstable character; that the mother is unable to train the child properly in her legacy; that the mother has a paramour, under whose protection and provision she is now residing, proving her immoral character; that the mother is too young and is barely of age; and that the child's father wished for his mother, the elder Mrs. Courtney, to care for the child in the event of his untimely death.

Though Mrs. Courtney likely has no proof of any of these accusations, she is likely to convince the Chancery to award her guardianship, as these are very weighty accusations and Mrs. Courtney has the means, obviously, to hire the best barristers.

Lillian's face began to tingle and her vision to go dark. Was she about to faint, like one of Nash's heroines in his novels?

"Sit down here." Lady Barrentine led her to a chair and seated her, while Lillian leaned forward and took deep breaths.

"Did you read the entire letter?"

Lillian shook her head.

"There was no need. I'm so sorry, but I want you to know that I have instructed my solicitor to send our own brief to another of the best barristers in London, and have him fight this in the Chancery. We shall fight this injustice, my dear, so do not worry. And with the backlog of cases, my solicitor assures me that it will not be decided for months to come."

Lady Barrentine had procured a paper fan from somewhere and was fanning Lillian's face with it.

"Are you all right, dear Lillian? I am so sorry to give you such a shock, but I thought you should know."

"Yes," Lillian managed to say. "Thank you for telling me."

"Do you have your own solicitor?"

"No." And she did not have the means to employ one either.

"Do not worry about that, for I shall have my solicitor work on your behalf, and the barrister he has chosen, he assures me, is just as good as Mrs. Courtney's." Lady Barrentine continued to speak, but Lillian did not hear what she was saying. Her mind was hazy and her thoughts were spinning at great speed through her head. Would she lose Bella after all?

"I hate to be the one to say it," Lady Barrentine was saying when Lillian was a bit calmer and could take heed to her words, "but the best way to protect yourself and to ensure Bella stays with you is to remarry."

"How would that help me?"

"A new husband could ensure that you are of stable, good moral character, and Mrs. Courtney wouldn't dare accuse you of having a lover. And your new husband could have himself declared Bella's guardian."

It seemed unfair that she needed to marry to prove

her worth, but such was society's rules.

"I cannot imagine who would marry me now. I don't have the inclination nor . . ."

"As lovely and sweet as you are, there are a great many men who would jump at the chance to marry you."

Lillian shook her head. "I am not in society enough, and my first marriage was so unhappy . . . but I should make sure Bella is not crying or making more work for your servants."

"Of course. We shall look in on the child." Lady Barrentine led the way.

When Bella saw Lillian, she held up a fist full of dough. "I'm making cakes!"

The maidservant helped her pat down the ball of dough onto a pan, then wiped her chubby fingers with a cloth. "There. All clean."

Bella held her arms out to her mother, and Lillian picked her up and held her close, the breath going out of her as she remembered the cruel way in which Bella might be taken from her, through the courts and through completely false accusations.

"Shall we go and have our tea?" Lady Barrentine asked.

"Thank you for watching Bella," Lillian said to the servants.

"She is a dear, sweet girl," the servant said.

"We'll send her cake to her when it's done," the cook said, shoving the pan into the oven as she spoke.

"You made a cake!" Lillian said, tears pooling in her eyes in spite of her best efforts.

"I made a cake!" Bella clapped her hands with a gleeful smile.

As Lillian managed to swallow a sip of her tea,

Lady Barrentine said, "You must tell yourself you will not worry. You are trusting Providence and trusting to me, your faithful friend, and to my barrister, to stop this evil plot, and all will be well. Don't let yourself think otherwise." Lady Barrentine nodded confidently.

It was a good plan, and since Lillian had no other, she decided to do her best to implement it.

And she did have another plan, she realized, as she told herself that if her mother-in-law seemed to be succeeding, she could find a man to marry, someone who wouldn't hit her or otherwise abuse her or Bella. That was about all she even hoped for, as she didn't have it in her to hope for some wonderful man who would love and cherish her.

But she could not lose Bella.

CHAPTER ELEVEN

A knock brought Lillian up short as she prepared a simple midday meal for herself and Bella, of bread she had baked, butter and cheese, as well as eggs and a buttery cheese sauce she had made herself, along with asparagus and potatoes from the kitchen garden.

"We are never able to eat all the garden produces," the cook and Lady Barrentine had both assured her, telling her to take as much as she and Bella could eat, whenever and whatever she wanted. And when Lillian was convinced that there were indeed some vegetables going to waste, uneaten, in the garden, she began to do as they bid.

Lillian discovered that she enjoyed cooking. There was something satisfying about taking foods and creating something that looked and tasted good, which would nourish and strengthen herself and her daughter.

She went to the door, expecting Lady Barrentine, and found Christopher standing there.

"How wonderful to see you," Lillian said. Her brother had come to visit her, and he did not appear to have been drinking. "Come in, please."

"I won't stay long. I was just riding through the area, on my way home."

"I am glad you stopped by. Bella will be happy to see her uncle."

Bella toddled in, and Christopher bent down to her. "Good day, little one," he said. "Is that a new doll you have there?" He pointed to the less ragged of the two dolls she held in her arms.

Bella didn't answer, just held her doll up for his inspection.

Lillian said, "Lady Barrentine gave her the doll just recently."

Christopher straightened up and spoke to Lillian. "We got your letter saying you were living here in the cottage. Do you not employ any servants? Why would you live this way, Lilly? You know, you and Bella have a home with us. You should come and stay with us, in your old childhood home, where you'd have servants and wouldn't have to stay on someone else's charity."

"Thank you. I don't mind the lack of servants, and I find I enjoy the solitude here. It's very peaceful, and Lady Barrentine has been very good to us. It's not charity, as I fully intend to pay for our lodgings."

Christopher just stared at the wall.

"I am just preparing a luncheon. You must join Bella and me. It is simple food, but good and filling, I daresay."

"I didn't come here to eat your food."

"Of course not, but you might as well eat with us."

"I have to get home. I just wanted to check in on you . . . I would take a bit of brandy if you have it."

"I'm so sorry. I don't have any brandy, or any spirits at all. But we can walk over to the main house and you can have a drink there, I'm sure." She regretted the suggestion as soon as she made it.

"I would not intrude on them. Is the earl home?"

"I believe he is."

"You know, there are rumors about you and him— not that I would judge you for it at all."

"Rumors?" Lillian felt her cheeks start to burn.

"That was one reason I called. You could prove the rumors are false if you come live with us in Hampshire. You would be good company for Gretchen, and Bella could be a good playmate for Priscilla as well."

"The rumors are false. I can't imagine why anyone . . . Anyone who would invent such a rumor is cruel and evil."

"I'm not arguing with you there, sis, but the truth is that people say terrible things, and they listen to rumors. Your reputation . . ."

"I know, I know." Lillian rubbed her forehead as a headache was starting there. "Let me think about it."

"Consider it. I can send a carriage for you."

"Thank you. I truly appreciate the offer, and I . . . I probably will come, at least for a visit, if that is all right with Gretchen."

"She would be glad to have the company."

They talked a few more minutes before Christopher took his leave and again refused to accept her invitation to stay and dine with her and Bella.

When he was gone, Lillian let out a deep sigh. She did not wish to go to her brother's house, but perhaps it would be best, in order to try and salvage her reputation. After all, she'd never get a husband and protector-guardian for Bella if her reputation was ruined by ridiculous rumors.

~ ~ ~

The weather was good, so Nash had decided to ride to the village of Gantt and speak to the constable again.

"I have a name," the constable said, after inviting Nash into his parlour. "John Reed. I didn't send you word, as I don't know for certain if he is the man who accosted Mrs. Lillian Courtney, but he was recently released from prison for robbery and was here, visiting a friend, he said, and he hasn't been seen in a while, not since Lillian Courtney left Stokemont Abbey."

"I see."

"And I would ask you not to tell Mrs. Courtney, nor anyone else, that I gave you this information."

"And why is that?"

"I got the impression," he said, lowering his already low voice so much that Nash could barely hear him, "that the elder Mrs. Courtney did not wish me to discover who the man was. And if that is the case, it would be best for me if she did not know I was looking for him or had given you this name."

"I shall not mention you to anyone, of course. It will be as if we had never spoken." Nash handed the man two ten-pound notes. "If you discover any more information, send me word."

"It might be best if you come here instead of waiting on me to send word. After all, everything I do can be found out."

"I understand."

He went away more determined than ever to find, apprehend, and force the man to tell him everything he knew, including who had hired him to attack Lillian.

His life was imitating his novels and those he satirized more and more every day, and it was like a huge sign right in front of him, although he did not yet know what the sign meant.

Nevertheless, the irony of his suddenly melodramatic life was not lost on him.

~ ~ ~

"Where are we going?" Bella asked for the second time, the carriage rocking back and forth.

"We're going for a visit to your uncle and aunt's house in Hampshire," Lillian explained again, "to your little cousin Priscilla's home. You remember visiting them before we came to live at our cottage."

Bella did not speak for a moment. Then she said, "Can I play with Priscilla's dolls?"

"You may share her dolls, and you will share your dolls with her."

Bella looked sad. "I don't think she will want to play with my dolls."

"But it's only fair, if you play with her dolls, you must let her play with yours."

Bella sighed, a long sigh as she stared down at her dolls, and soon fell asleep leaning against her mother's side.

Lillian stretched out Bella's legs on the seat, laying Bella's head on Lillian's lap.

When they arrived, only the housekeeper was there to greet them.

"I'm afraid Mr. and Mrs. Hartman are not at home," the housekeeper said, "but I shall show you to your room. The footmen will bring your trunks."

"Thank you." She didn't bother to say that she'd only brought one trunk, not planning to stay longer than a week.

Lillian always felt uneasy here, but she felt even

more so now. Why were her brother and sister-in-law absent? She'd written to say they were coming. The housekeeper seemed to be expecting them.

Bella's nap had been short, so they both lay down on the bed and fell asleep.

A knock on the door awakened them.

"Mr. and Mrs. Hartman are downstairs," the servant said, "and wish to know if you are coming down for tea."

"Yes, we shall be down in a few moments."

Bella clung to Lillian's neck as they went down the stairs. Lillian spoke soothingly to her.

Gretchen greeted them with a huge smile, which turned into a smirk. "Forgive us for not being here to greet you. We were indisposed."

A glance at the clock told Lillian that barely half an hour had passed since she and Bella had arrived.

"I trust your journey was uneventful," Christopher said.

"It was, I thank you." Bella was clinging so tightly to Lillian's neck that her voice came out sounding slightly strangled.

"Christopher and I were invited to dine at Sir Dauncey's home an hour away by carriage, and Christopher has secured an invitation for you too, but I'm afraid you will have to leave Bella at home for this kind of dinner party. I hope you don't mind." She smirked and laid a hand on Christopher's leg. "I don't like to leave Priscilla here either, as she is my constant companion and clings to me just as Bella does to you, but Sir Dauncey is a baronet and his wife the daughter of a viscount, and they are very strict and formal about following the little unwritten rules of society. I know you understand what I mean, as you are now living with an earl."

"I am not living with an earl. Lady Barrentine allows me to pay for lodgings on the grounds—"

"Oh, yes, of course, but you know my meaning. These great ladies and lords are very particular about what they do, as everyone is so quick to talk, talk, talk about their every action, and we must mind our reputations. Heaven forbid something should happen to my husband—to Christopher—but if he were gone, I would have to find another husband, and my reputation would then be my most important possession. You know that, of course, better than I do. And so we must obey the rules of society, I suppose."

There was no need for Lillian to speak, as Gretchen continued on and on. Lillian often told herself that Gretchen meant no harm. After all, anyone who talked as much as Gretchen did was bound to say things that might sound offensive. Nevertheless, it was difficult to listen to her speak of painful things as if they were no more distressing or unusual than a foggy morning or a misplaced glove.

In the evening, Lillian reluctantly left Bella in the care of Priscilla's nurse while the two cousins played together on the floor.

She had no wish to go to a dinner party with strangers, but the whole point of visiting Christopher and Gretchen was to stifle the rumors about her and Lord Barrentine, so it was important to be seen in society.

The dinner party was seven couples, Lillian having been paired with an elderly widower whose wife had died the year before. Thankfully, he was quiet and respectful and did not try to flirt with her, but talked mostly of his children and grandchildren, which allowed her to talk of Bella.

During the last course of the dinner, her dinner partner said, "And do not worry, my dear, about what Mrs. Courtney is saying about you and the Earl of Barrentine. She must have her way, so you may have to placate her by letting her have guardianship of the child. You are young. You will get married and have more children."

Lillian's heart constricted so painfully at his words that, for a moment, she couldn't speak. Finally, she said, "I am not sure what you mean. Mrs. Courtney spoke to you about me?"

"She was in London a few days ago, as was I, on the last day of my stay there, and we saw each other at a party such as this one. She was speaking rather rudely about you, my dear, and suggesting that you were staying at Dunbridge Hall because of a dalliance between you and Lord Barrentine, but we all knew she was only speaking out of the bitterness of a woman who had lost her child to an early death. Nevertheless, you must be careful, my dear. To make an enemy of a woman like Mrs. Courtney is to bring down a lot of trouble on one's head."

"I cannot just give her guardianship of my child." Lillian's breath was coming in restricted gasps.

"You can, or she will take the child from you and have you declared unfit. She is already threatening to do so, unless I'm mistaken. Forgive me. I see I have upset you, but I'm only speaking as I would to my own daughters."

Did the man not understand that Bella was the only person in the world who brought even a tiny bit of happiness and joy to her life?

More importantly, the man surely understood that to give her away to Mrs. Courtney was to give her over to a heartless woman who had turned her own son into a monster who was overbearing and abusive to his own wife. Lillian could not and would allow her to get control over Bella.

She said nothing more to the man and hardly spoke the rest of the evening, her heart heavy and her feelings numb. How many people at the dinner party would have said the same thing—that she should give her daughter up to save her reputation from being shredded by the bitter and hateful Mrs. Courtney?

She was in for a difficult battle, but one she had to win.

~ ~ ~

When their visit with Christopher and Gretchen was over, Lillian journeyed back to Dunbridge Hall with a measure of relief that was nearly snuffed out by the fear and anxiety that had kept her awake at night and so clouded her mind that she could barely pray more than a frenzied, "Help me, God. Please help me."

As if sensing her mother's emotional state, Bella clung to Lillian more than usual. But once they were back in their cottage, they both were able to relax a bit.

Lillian had decided to swallow her pride, as well as her guilt, and accept whatever help Lady Barrentine and her son Nash might offer. She truly was that desperate to save her daughter.

CHAPTER TWELVE

Nash listened as his mother told him what Lillian had told her, what she'd learned from the guests of a dinner party she'd attended, and exactly why she feared allowing Mrs. Courtney to get control of Bella.

"The things she told me were really strange," Mother said. "I told you that she said her husband struck her on two different occasions, but she told me that one of those occasions was in the presence of Mrs. Courtney and Bella. In fact, she was holding Bella in her arms when he struck her in the back, actually shoving her to the floor, and it was all she could do to keep from falling on Bella or dropping her."

Nash's blood started to boil. How dare that man?

"Lillian avows that Mrs. Courtney saw him strike her but said nothing to her son, only said. 'This is why everyone should employ a nurse,' or some such thing, blaming Lillian because her husband became angry enough to strike her in the back. And it was after the second time he struck her in the back that she ran away from him to the Isle of Wight. He followed her there and that's where he fell off a cliff and died."

Nash's face was hot, and he could feel his blood pumping through his limbs. If that evil Courtney was still alive, Nash would have loved to smash a fist into his face.

"I always hated him when we were in school," Nash admitted.

They'd attended the same school for a couple of years, and Courtney had always done whatever was necessary to make the more popular, more aggressive boys like him and include him in their circles. Once, Courtney and his friends had sneaked away from school with some older boys to smoke and drink brandy. Nash refused to lie for them and tell the instructor that they were all sick or studying in their rooms. So they found Nash when he was reading alone in his room. Though Nash had fought back, there were too many of them, and they had beaten him bloody.

Nash hadn't told the instructor anything, only said he didn't know where Courtney was, which was true enough. But those boys, including Courtney, beat him for it.

He wished he could confront Courtney now about what he'd done to his wife and daughter. He'd tell him he didn't deserve a wife or a child. He might even challenge him to a duel with swords, as he'd become quite good at fencing and practiced often. He'd love to see fear in the man's eyes and hear him swear never to strike a woman again.

"Poor Lillian. She didn't deserve to be treated so." Mother's lip quivered and she pressed her hand against her mouth.

It was true. Lillian deserved a husband who would take care of her, love her, and treat her well, someone who would appreciate her for all her good qualities, including her courage, her intelligence, and her great love for her child. Admittedly, he didn't know her very well, but he knew her well enough to know that she deserved someone infinitely better than Courtney.

And as for Courtney's mother, if she were a man, he'd go and demand that she cease spreading lies about her former daughter-in-law and himself. But as Mrs. Courtney was a woman, there was very little he could do or say.

"We must fight Mrs. Courtney through the law," Mother was saying. "We must solicit the court's favor and hope . . ." Mother sighed.

"What?"

"Well, as we are completely unrelated to Lillian and Bella, there really is so little that we can do. We can provide the finances for her to hire the best barrister, but the courts will care little about our opinion or our assertions. And as a young woman, without powerful connections or fortune, her best hope is . . ."

Nash already knew what his mother was going to say. "Her best hope is to marry a gentleman, someone who will commit to the guardianship of the child."

"Now, don't think I am suggesting that gentleman is you," Mother was quick to say. "But yes. That is her best hope. And she must do it quickly, before Mrs. Courtney is able to take her case before the Court of Chancery."

If he married her, all her problems would be solved —she would no longer have to worry about gossips destroying her reputation, and most of all, she wouldn't have to worry about Mrs. Courtney taking her daughter away from her. But would she even want to marry him?

"Darling." Mother touched his arm, wrenching him

from his thoughts. "You are generous and noble, and I have always been proud of those qualities in you. But please don't think you have to marry Lillian to save her, not if you were hoping to marry someone else. Be mindful of whether you might regret such a step."

"Of course, Mother." He said no more. But he was actually thinking that he was afraid he might regret *not* marrying Lillian and not saving her.

Saving her? Once again, his life was imitating his books, and he was fairly certain he should be disgusted with himself. But should he be disgusted with his real self, or his writing self?

~ ~ ~

Lillian recalled the conversation she'd had with her brother when Gretchen wasn't around. He'd advised her, "Marry Lord Barrentine. He's rich and powerful, I would imagine. He could keep old Mrs. Courtney away from Bella. No doubt he could find barristers as greedy and grasping as Mrs. Courtney's."

"I cannot very well just go and marry Lord Barrentine." Lillian gave her brother what she hoped was a shocked and incredulous look.

"You ladies know how to flirt and turn a man's head. I'm sure you could get him if you set your mind to it."

"I suppose I'm not that kind of lady, because I wouldn't know how to do that." And did she really want to "get" a husband that way?

Under normal circumstances she would not, but . . . was she desperate enough to "set her mind to getting" Lord Barrentine?

Certainly, there was no unmarried man of her acquaintance whom she would rather marry, but she actually did not know Nash—Lord Barrentine—very well. At the same time, she had no worries that he might hit her or mistreat Bella.

She also hadn't thought her husband, Bella's father, would ever do such things either. She'd been so naïve then, and if she was honest, she was probably still naïve. And that was what was so frightening. What if she made the same mistake again?

But Lady Barrentine would never stand for Nash mistreating them. There was no strangeness, no aggression and darkness between Nash and his mother, as there was between Lillian's first husband and Mrs. Courtney, and Lillian did feel as if she knew Lady Barrentine very well. She'd spent time with her every day they'd been at the cottage at Dunbridge Hall.

The weather was so pleasant that Lillian and Bella took their midday meal outside to enjoy a picnic in the flower garden.

"Mamma, it's Lord Barrentine."

Lillian turned in the direction Bella was pointing and saw Nash walking toward them.

"Good afternoon, ladies," he said.

"Good afternoon," they said, squinting up at him. "Please, join our picnic," Lillian said with a smile, suddenly feeling shy, her cheeks warming, as she remembered her conversation with her brother.

"Don't let me disturb you," he said.

Bella cried, "Come and sit by me!"

Nash did as she bade him, sitting down on the edge of their blanket. He stretched his long legs out to the side.

"I finished your book while I was visiting my brother, and I quite enjoyed it," Lillian said. "It made me laugh out loud more than once."

"I thank you." He looked slightly uncomfortable. "Forgive me. I'm not accustomed to receiving compliments on my novels."

"Only because no one knew you wrote them until recently. But I am certain you will become accustomed to it, as so many people will be reading your books." She smiled. "Indeed, it is rare that a book takes my mind completely off my own thoughts and troubles, but yours did."

"You are too kind."

"I only speak the truth. I do not lie."

"You never lie?"

"I have many faults," she said, "but I believe that I may safely say that lying is not one of them. And you?"

"My faults, I suppose, are that I am too taciturn, and I am a bit selfish and self-absorbed. I can be quite thoughtless." He paused a moment, then said, "Now, have I put you off? Will you not wish to be my friend now that you know these things about me?"

"Well, I may be young and inexperienced in the world, but I do believe it is the man who never realizes he is selfish and thoughtless who is truly thoughtless. The man who recognizes those traits in himself cannot be too terribly bad."

"So, the truly evil man will never admit to any faults. Is that what you're saying?"

Lillian remembered how her husband, before they were married, had insisted upon the fact that he was a good man, that he did not do the bad things that other men did—he did not have paramours or engage in seductions, did not gamble away his family fortune or drink himself into unconsciousness. In fact, he had told her many times, even after they were married, that he was a good man, and never did he admit to any faults or shortcomings.

"May I go pick some flowers, Mamma?" Bella asked.

Lillian picked up a cloth and wiped the crumbs from Bella's mouth. "Yes you may."

When Bella had walked a few feet away, Lillian was still thinking about what Nash had said, how he had self-deprecatingly listed his own faults. Lillian said, "The good man examines himself and understands that he is not innately good, though he strives to be, while the evil man believes that he is good, and he ignores his faults because he has no intention of striving to overcome them. Perhaps?"

"I think you have phrased it just right. In fact, I believe there are some men who believe they have no faults, thus proving that they are full of them."

They both smiled, as if amused.

"We are philosophers," Lillian jested.

"Indeed. But in all seriousness, I do believe you understand. But then, it is hard to find a man who is not wise in his own eyes."

"Yes, but some men are so obtuse . . ." She was about to say something about her dead husband, and that did not seem very charitable.

"Yes?"

"Nothing." She shook her head.

They were quiet as they watched Bella, who had wandered away from the flower garden to, ironically, pick the wildflowers growing nearby.

"Forgive me if I am prying, but Mother explained to me that your former husband was not a very good man, and certainly was not good to you."

Her heart rose into her throat. The same feeling of shame swept over her that she had felt when her husband had struck her and shoved her to the floor. She remembered how she had caught herself with her hand to keep from falling on Bella. But Lord Barrentine had not witnessed that. He'd only heard what his mother had told him, which was only what Lillian had told her.

"He was not a very attentive husband," Lillian said softly. "In fact, I felt as if he hated me." Perhaps that was the worst part of all, worse even than being struck by him; the pain of being ignored was far worse and more lingering than the pain of being struck.

Tears pricked her eyes. Why was she confessing this to Nash? "Forgive me. You couldn't possibly want to hear about any of this."

"I want to hear anything you wish to tell me."

His voice was so gentle, so caring, it took her breath away. She stared at the ground, trying to control her breathing, as she couldn't bear to look him in the eye. He might even see the tears there.

"No man should ever strike his wife," Nash said softly. "It is wrong and against several laws, especially God's law. Courtney did not deserve you or Bella."

Lillian glanced up at him, and their eyes met in a way that sent a jolt all the way down to her toes. She had to swallow past a lump in her throat before she could speak.

"You are very kind to say so." Her voice was so breathy, she wondered if he could hear her.

"It is the truth. And if I were your husband, I would treat you and Bella with nothing but gentleness. No one would ever hurt you again."

What was he saying? If he was her husband?

"Lillian Courtney, will you do me the greatest honor in agreeing to marry me?"

Her stomach leapt and flipped inside her. Never did she dream that Nash, the Earl of Barrentine, had ever had one thought about marrying her. But would he love her and Bella? She so wanted to be loved.

Suddenly the desire nearly overwhelmed her. And just as abruptly, a wave of fear swept over her. She'd hoped and believed her first husband would love her. Would she be just as unfortunate this time? After all, he'd said nothing at all about love.

And yet . . . he'd promised to treat her and Bella with nothing but gentleness. That was what he said. And he could certainly protect her and Bella from Mrs. Courtney's schemes.

"Yes, I will," she breathed.

They were both still seated on the blanket as Bella picked flowers and sang softly to herself.

Nash moved closed enough to take her hand. He drew it to his lips and kissed it, the first time he had ever done so.

His touch, warm and gentle, yet firm, sent a thrill straight to her heart.

"I shall endeavor to be worthy of your love," he said solemnly, looking her in the eye, still holding her hand.

Bella ran toward them with a fist full of flowers. "Look, Mamma! I picked these for you!" She climbed into Lillian's lap as Nash released her hand.

"They are very beautiful," Lillian said.

"Well, I shall leave you now. Shall I see you tonight? That is, will you dine with us?"

"Yes, I thank you." Her stomach was doing its flipping and flopping again.

He nodded to her, turned on his heel, and strode away.

Had that truly just happened? Had Nash Golding, Lord Barrentine, asked her to marry him?

Her heart beat like a horse kicking her in the ribs. All sorts of fears began to attack her. What if he regretted asking her? After all, his proposal of marriage did not sound very rehearsed or planned. What if he found he couldn't love her and Bella? Or what if his sisters were so angry that they persecuted her continuously, hating her for "trapping" their brother? Or, worse than that, what if Lady Barrentine was unhappy with his choice and ceased to be her friend?

But another feeling was also present, and that was a feeling of happiness at the thought of being wanted and cared for by Nash Golding.

Just as quickly it was replaced by fear again, that her second marriage would be too similar to her first. *O God, help me.*

At least, if she married Nash, he would make sure nothing happened to Bella. In fact, that might be exactly why he was asking her to marry him. What if he was only trying to help her? What if he never intended to love her?

God, please take these torturous thoughts from me.

CHAPTER THIRTEEN

Nash felt his heart pounding sickeningly as he walked away from Lillian and Bella, back toward the main house. He had just become engaged, and very quickly and abruptly, without taking much time to truly think it over.

He'd prayed just that morning about whether he should ask Lillian to marry him. But he had not intended to ask her today. He'd only intended to talk with her when he saw her and Bella outside. Was he truly so impulsive?

And yet, a part of him did not regret it at all. A part of him felt quite at peace. A lovely woman—lovely both inside and out, a good woman with whom he enjoyed conversing—had just agreed to marry him.

Lillian. When he had kissed her hand, he'd felt something he'd never felt before, and his thoughts had gone to kissing her lips.

When he did kiss her, would she be disappointed at his complete inexperience? Would she dislike being married to him?

No, he wouldn't think like that. After all, she'd been

married to that fiend, Courtney. Nash's love would easily win her over after that man's cruelty.

He was only a few steps away from the house when his mother came out the door.

"Nash, dear, I was just about to take this letter to Lillian and Bella."

"It's not from Mrs. Courtney?"

"No, no, the direction on the back says Lincolnshire. Probably a friend or relative. Are you well, my dear? You look flushed." Mother leaned toward him with a look of concern.

"I am perfectly well, but I have something important to tell you. Come inside a moment."

They both stepped inside and Nash led her into a small sitting room in a quiet corner of the house.

"What is it? Is something wrong?"

"No, not at all." He tried to think of the best way to tell her, but he ended up simply blurting out, "I have asked Lillian to marry me, and we are engaged."

Mother's eyes widened as she stared at him in silence.

"I know it must seem sudden, but it is the only way to ensure Bella is not taken from her mother."

"Son, you are not marrying her out of charity, are you? For I'm sure we could find a suitable match for her. In fact, I was just thinking of eligible men—"

"No, Mother. That will not do." No respectable man of fortune worth having would wish to be "set up" to marry a poor widow in order to save her child. No one worthy of Lillian, certainly. "I am marrying her."

"But is there an attachment on your side? You should not marry without love and respect."

"I am attached. She is my choice."

"Well, you could hardly do better than sweet, sensible Lillian, and I believe you will be happy, but I do dread to hear what your sisters will say."

"They shall come round eventually, I daresay." Nash said wryly.

"Yes, you are right, they will." Mother took a deep breath and squeezed his arm. "I am very happy for you both."

"Thank you, Mother." That had gone much better than he'd feared. "And I believe I must send something to her home parish so that the banns can be read?"

"Oh, no, dear. You should get a license. I can help with the preparations. But you don't want the banns to be called, at your parish as well as hers, for three weeks. A license is preferable. We don't wish to have a lot of gossip, especially from Mrs. Courtney, while we wait the three Sundays for the banns to be called. You may get an ordinary license and be married right away."

"There is no great hurry, I suppose."

"No, but you mustn't wait until Mrs. Courtney has managed to get a ruling from the Court of Chancery."

"No, I don't want to wait that long."

"You can ask our own clergyman to issue a common license, and you and Lillian shall write a sworn statement saying there are no impediments to your marriage. After you get the license, you will have two weeks to get married." Mother's smile grew bigger the longer she spoke. Finally, she clasped her hands together and sighed, looking quite pleased.

"Very well. If Lillian is in agreement, we can get married as soon as she wishes."

"May I go and speak to her about it?"

"I suppose."

First, his secret identity as Perceval Hastings, satirical novel writer, had been revealed to the world, bringing attention, criticism, and ridicule, and now he was getting married to someone he had known for only a few weeks.

Where had his quiet life gone? And was it lost forever? Either way, there was no going back now.

~ ~ ~

Lillian had decided that if Lord Barrentine sent her a note saying he'd acted hastily in asking her to marry him that she would let him out of the engagement. But when Lady Barrentine came excitedly asking Lillian to set the date for the wedding, she knew Nash had been serious about asking her to marry him. He would not have told his mother of their engagement if he regretted having asked her.

She was truly marrying Nash Golding.

Lady Barrentine insisted they marry quickly. "The sooner the better," she said. "Nash said he is ready to marry as soon as you wish, and it does need to be soon, my dear. You want to make certain you are able to petition the court to grant Nash—your husband—full guardianship of Bella before Mrs. Courtney is able to dispute it."

"Next week, then?"

"Yes, that is good. Nash will see the rector and get a license so you don't have to wait for the banns to be called. Best not to give Mrs. Courtney an idea that you are getting married. It will be hard enough keeping it a secret with my daughters here. Did I tell you? My other unmarried daughter, Emma, is arriving today."

Lillian's heart sank. What would Nash's sisters say about him marrying a penniless widow with a child? No doubt they would scold their brother for his unreasonable charity. They might even persuade him not to marry her.

An hour ago, she was having bouts of fear at the thought of marrying again. Now she was terrified he might change his mind.

CHAPTER FOURTEEN

When Lillian and Bella arrived for dinner, walking into the sitting room where the rest of the family was already gathered, Nash's newly-arrived sister saw Bella and gasped.

"Oh, the pretty little thing!" she cried.

Lady Barrentine quickly made the introductions, and the usual mannerly greetings were said.

"Oh, Mamma, you told me she was pretty and sweet, but I have never seen such a beautiful little girl." Thankfully, Emma kept her voice low, and Bella didn't realize she was being spoken about or she would have crawled up Lillian's body like a squirrel and wrapped her arms around her neck, as she did whenever she was unsure of the people around her.

At the moment Bella was focused on Lady Barrentine, who was smiling and holding her arms out.

"There's my favorite little girl," Lady Barrentine said, while Bella went to her waiting arms.

Emma wisely didn't make any sudden movements. She must have had experience with young children like

Bella, who were often as shy and skittish as any deer in the forest. But Bella warmed up to her fairly quickly, as Emma talked quietly to her and offered her a biscuit she'd brought from the kitchen.

Meanwhile, Mildred was sitting with her arms folded, her nose tilted at a superior angle upwards. She said not a word and barely glanced at Bella. Finally, she murmured, "Truly, Emma, you act as if you've never seen a child before."

Nash seemed not to notice anything that was happening, and he got up from his seat and moved closer to Lillian.

Her heart fluttered, but she was surprised at how calm she felt. He had already asked her to marry him, so what did she have to be nervous about? The wedding was in seven days, and there was very little that needed to be done to prepare for it. The most frightening part was facing his disapproving sisters. Did they know of their engagement? Lady Barrentine certainly was happy about it. *Thank you, God.*

Nash began to talk to her in an unassuming voice while the others in the room were busy talking to Bella. "I have taken the liberty of asking our clergyman, Mr. Barlow, for a license to marry. And Mother has told me that you are happy with marrying on the seventeenth."

"Yes." Lillian smiled. Looking him in the eye made her heart flutter again, so she looked down.

Was she truly about to marry this man seven days hence? It seemed unreal, and yet, there was something almost . . . familiar about their engagement, as if she'd known for some time that he would be her husband someday. But that was silly.

"I hear that I am to congratulate you on getting engaged to my brother," Mildred said suddenly, but the expression on her face did not look congratulatory; her eyes were cold.

"We are engaged to be married," Nash answered just as coldly, relieving Lillian from having to figure out how to reply to his sister's unfriendly statement.

"Yes, and I am congratulating her."

"I am the one to be congratulated," Nash said. "I am gaining not only an exceptional wife but also a wonderful daughter. And so, I thank you for your congratulations."

"Well, I was not congratulating you. I was congratulating your future wife."

"I thank you," Lillian said quickly, hoping to put a halt to the cold back-and-forth.

Nash glared at his sister. Lillian held her breath, but when he did not speak again, she let it out.

"Oh yes," Emma said, as if she had not just heard her brother and sister's exchange. "I am very happy for you, Lillian, and for my brother. It will be good having someone to force my brother to be sociable, especially now that everyone is laughing at him for publishing his funny stories."

Nash let out a long sigh and sat back against the sofa.

"I thank you." Lillian was hard-pressed to suppress a laugh. "As for people laughing at him, it is only a short-lived fracas perpetuated by the many London newspapers to make money off a sensational story. But an earl writing novels is not a big enough story to sell their papers for very long. They will soon cease to write about it, and I'm sure everyone will have forgotten all about it by the time Parliament is in session again. There will be a new scandal by then."

The sisters and Lady Barrentine all stopped what they were doing to listen to Lillian's little speech. Even Nash stopped his brooding long enough to look at her.

"Well said, darling," Lady Barrentine said. "You are absolutely right. No one will remember it in six months."

"But I shall write more novels," Nash observed matter-of-factly. "And each time one releases to the public, more will be said about an earl writing novels. The challenge for me, and for my wife," he added, glancing at Lillian, "is to not care what the newspapers write or what the people say."

"Yes, very true." Lillian was quick to give him an assured smile, lifting her chin to show her confidence in him.

But in truth, her heart sank at the thought of so much derision and attention aimed toward her husband, more for his sake than her own, as she could imagine how it would bother him.

Bella—and Lillian—would be happy to have a stable home again, and Nash's guardianship would protect them from Mrs. Courtney. And she and Nash would become accustomed to the things people would say and would learn to ignore them.

"Surely you aren't going to publish more novels," Mildred said. "Were the first two so well-received, so lucrative, that you would dare the peerage's censorship over and over again?"

"I am surprised as well," Lady Barrentine said. "Why not just write them and not publish them?"

Her future husband's face was turning a light shade of red. "Must we discuss this tonight?"

"I agree with Nash," Emma said. "Lillian will think she is marrying into the most contentious family in England."

"Yes, let us talk of pleasant things, like the wedding. You will both be there, and I have already written to your sister Ophelia to come."

"She won't come," Mildred said. "She is having such a pleasant time in London, she won't tear herself away for a wedding."

"Cook and I are planning the food for after the wedding. Lillian, is there anything you would like to add to the menu? What are your favorite foods?"

Lillian listed a few foods that she enjoyed, then said, "You have an excellent cook, so I am sure it will all be wonderful."

Gradually the conversation shifted to other things, much to Lillian's relief, and then Mildred began to play the pianoforte quite expertly, causing their faces to relax into much more cheerful expressions.

Everyone, that is, except for Nash. He still looked quite put out. And that thought led her to think, *Would he become easily put out with me? Or worse, with Bella? Would he turn out to be like Bella's father?*

Her breath shallowed. Surely she was only being paranoid. Nash did not remind her of her first husband at all, and his anger toward his sister Mildred was quite understandable. Still, it was impossible not to feel some fear. The last thing she wanted was to make the same mistake again, marrying a man who neither loved her nor treated her well.

Dinner progressed more pleasantly, with Mildred and Emma conversing mostly with each other, as they had not seen each other in weeks, while Lady Barrentine, Nash, and Lillian carried on a pleasant conversation about many topics.

"I very much enjoy musical recitals," Lillian answered Lady Barrentine's query. "I also enjoy theatricals. Do you like those things?" she asked Nash.

"I do."

"I know you enjoy architecture. You must have some favorite places in London."

"I like reading about their history. I actually prefer the older castles, which one can find in the countryside, more than any London buildings. Except, perhaps, the buildings of the Tower of London."

"Oh, yes, the white tower is magnificent."

"And some of the other old buildings, dating from before the fifteenth century."

"Yes, those are my favorites too. But you must admit, London has some beautiful old churches and cathedrals."

"The oldest ones are the best."

She could see that he was beginning to enjoy the conversation, especially when he began to tell a story about something that happened during the planning and creation of one of the towers in the Tower of London complex of buildings. His blue eyes actually sparkled in the candlelight and his whole body began to look more alive.

She imagined him coming alive like that for her, because he was in love with her. What would it be like to be loved by him? For him to become as enamored with her as he was with medieval architecture?

It would certainly be an experience unlike anything she'd ever had with her first husband.

She suppressed the thought, suddenly afraid someone might read her mind.

She became aware of Mildred and Emma's silent attention on their brother.

"Forgive me," Nash said. "I am talking too much about something most people find very dull." He might have made the statement with a bitter or a sarcastic tone, but instead, he said it in an endearingly humble way.

"I don't find it dull at all," Lillian said, aware that all eyes were on her. "I enjoy hearing about historical structures, and Lord Barrentine has an enthusiastic way of telling about them that makes it even more interesting."

Lady Barrentine and Emma bestowed big smiles on her, and even Mildred looked less coldly at her. And she imagined that Nash, though he avoided looking at her, appreciated her compliments.

Did Nash's sisters know he was mostly marrying her to save her and Bella from Mrs. Courtney? Lady Barrentine certainly knew, or at least suspected. Perhaps the most unselfish thing Lillian could do would be to break off the engagement. But she did wish to be a good wife to him. In fact, she was quite sure, since she had loved her first husband, she would have no trouble loving Nash. He was a good and kind gentleman.

Unless she was mistaken about him.

"Besides his dull conversation about old buildings, what else do you admire about my brother?" Mildred had a sly look on her face, which she quickly hid with a fake smile.

"Mildred." Nash's tone was a warning.

"Mildred, can we not have a pleasant dinner?" Lady Barrentine's eyes held their own, though gentler, warning.

"Is that not a fair and pleasant question to ask a newly engaged couple?" Mildred insisted.

"It is a fair question," Lillian said, "and I don't mind answering. I admire Nash's—that is, Lord Barrentine's—

kindness, his writing ability and way of telling a story, his forthrightness, his respectful and kind manner toward his mother, and most of all, his good character."

She could feel Nash's gaze on her. She dared to turn her head and meet his gaze. When she did, there was such a tenderness in his expression, and an intensity in his eyes, she felt herself blushing.

Were they just playing a part to impress his sisters? Or was his intense gaze a result of real feelings? The way her heart was pounding, *yearning*, was real enough.

"And what do you admire about Lillian?" Lady Barrentine said softly.

He took his eyes off Lillian to look at his mother. As he began to speak, Lillian forced herself to ignore the look of slight disgust on Mildred's face.

"The first thing I noticed and admired about her was that she was a kind and attentive mother. She is also kind and attentive to you, Mother."

She could see that his words did not impress Mildred, but he did not seem to notice.

"Lillian is gentle and has a cheerful nature, in spite of all the injustices life had dealt her."

Lillian could have disputed this with him, but she was more focused on the way he said her Christian name. She'd never heard him call her Lillian before, and it made her heart flutter like butterflies in her chest.

"She is courageous and humble, doing what she must, within moral confines, to care for her daughter. She is also a generous listener and conversationalist, and she is not proud or self-seeking. And the best and most important thing about her is her good character."

Lillian was gazing up at him, and when he turned and looked her in the eye to make these last statements, she felt something shift inside her—almost a magical feeling, a buoying up of her spirit, her heart expanding in her chest. She suddenly knew.

I am in love with Nash Golding.

CHAPTER FIFTEEN

Nash was very aware of his mother and two sisters staring at him, judging the both of them and whether they should be getting married—the same thing he'd been judging himself for. But Lillian's gentle but sincere-sounding praise of him settled it in his mind—he was doing the right thing.

And he suddenly realized as he was praising her —everything he was saying, he could say honestly. He might not have known her a long time, but he had already discovered so many good traits in her. Indeed, unless he was greatly mistaken, she would make a very good wife.

And the way Lillian was gazing up at him made him even more sure—and made him glad the wedding was only a week away.

Mother wiped a tear from her cheek, but her smile assured him that her tears were happy ones. She seemed to have difficulty speaking, swallowing and taking a breath before saying, "I am so very happy for you both. And for me! I have another wonderful daughter, and a sweet granddaughter in Bella. My dear, you don't mind me saying that, do you? Claiming Bella as my grand-daughter?"

"Of course not. It makes me very happy."

He could see the tears swimming in Lillian's eyes as well. And as he had learned as a boy, he was empathetic enough to struggle not to cry when he saw others crying. And as he had also learned as a boy, such a thing was not acceptable for a gentleman and peer of the realm. So he fought them back, staring down at his plate to clear his mind.

At least all these compliments and joy had shut his sister up. Mildred had nothing to say.

They finished their dessert in silence. He noticed Mother surreptitiously wiping her eyes a couple of times, so he tried not to stare in her direction. All the while, he was more aware than ever of Lillian sitting beside him, so close he could easily touch her, this fascinating woman who had endured so many things in such a short period of time, this lovely, gentle, good woman.

He'd been thinking how fortunate any penniless widow would be, as there were many of them in England, to marry him, a gentleman of large fortune, not to mention an earl and peer of the realm. Besides that, he considered himself to be a good man, of high morals. Certainly he would never strike his wife, as Lillian's first husband had done.

But he was just as fortunate. A good woman was not so easy to find. And he had no doubt he could love Bella as if she were his own daughter.

Truly, his mother was right. They were destined to be very happy.

As long as he could get past his insecurity about his inexperience. He had never even kissed a woman before.

But he disliked his insecurity. Or perhaps it would be better described as pride—not wishing to be seen as less than competent.

When the evening was over and Lillian announced that she would go upstairs and retrieve the sleeping Bella, Mother spoke up.

"Why don't you and Bella spend the night here?"

"It is all right. She doesn't even wake up when I carry her home and put her to bed."

"I insist. We can send for your things, whatever you need for the night. That way you won't have to disturb Bella at all. And in seven days, you will be spending all your nights here."

He thought he saw Lillian blushing.

"Very well."

Mother started up the stairs with Lillian.

Nash would have liked to have a moment alone with her, to walk her up to her room and at least kiss her hand. After all they'd said that evening in front of almost his entire family, he was rather looking forward to bidding her a good night in private. But as he watched her and his mother walking up the stairs, talking as they went, he told himself he'd have many opportunities in the future to privately bid her a good night.

~ ~ ~

Lillian awakened the next morning and stretched. Bella was asleep in a small child's bed next to hers, which the servants had moved into her room.

"So you and Bella don't disturb each other," Lady Barrentine said.

She had to admit, it was good to have the bed all to herself for the first time since she'd been staying at the cottage.

She felt herself smiling as she hummed her favorite song, which Mildred had played and sung the evening before. Perhaps if she had known it was Lillian's favorite, she wouldn't have chosen it. Lillian smiled wider and opened the curtains to let in the beautiful sunlight.

The servant entered the room. "You're up early," the servant said shyly.

"It is a beautiful morning."

"It is, mum. Lord Barrentine has already gone for a ride."

Lillian felt strangely let down at hearing this. She hadn't realized until that moment how much she'd been looking forward to seeing him at breakfast.

Bella awoke, immediately sat up, and looked around. "Mamma."

"I'm here." She lifted her daughter into her arms. "We spent the night at the main house. Isn't this a pretty room?" She took her over to the window to look out.

"I see our flowers." Bella pointed at the flower garden and wildflowers, far to the left, which were behind the dowager cottage.

Lillian decided not to try to explain to Bella that they would be staying at the main house, as it seemed more than Bella needed to know at the moment. Better to let her gradually become accustomed to being at the main house.

There were several matters, she realized, that she needed to discuss with Nash, pertaining to Bella especially. But perhaps she should not try to figure things out all at once. It was enough that Bella would have Nash for her guardian. Besides, their relationship felt fragile still.

~ ~ ~

For the next few days, Lillian and Bella spent very

little time at the cottage, as Lady Barrentine seemed to find reasons for them to stay at the main house. She had her seamstress making dresses for both Lillian and Bella to wear to the wedding.

"And you know, there will be many fittings as she makes the dresses."

There was also tea and meals, for which Lady Barrentine insisted she come to the main house. Lillian found herself often in Nash's company and the company of his mother and two sisters. But not once was she alone with Nash, just the two of them, for the next five days.

If they continued like this, the first time they would be alone would be on their wedding night.

The day before their wedding, Lillian had just put Bella down for her nap and gone downstairs. Lady Barrentine appeared at the bottom of the stairs.

"There you are, my dear. Did you already put Bella to sleep? Do let Emma and I take charge of her for the rest of the day. You know how much Emma and I enjoy Bella's company, and I believe Nash wanted to take you for a ride."

"You don't need me for any fittings?"

"No, dear. Your dress is mostly finished. She's working on Bella's dress today. Go on and enjoy yourself for the rest of the day."

Just then, she heard someone close the outside door closest to the stables, and the unmistakable sound of Nash's boots on the marble floor.

The now-familiar rush of anticipation at seeing him, the excitement of knowing that he would direct his gaze toward her first whenever he walked into the room, came over her. He would have a particular tender tone in his voice when he greeted her, as compared to his greeting to his sisters and mother. Already she knew these pleasant things about him.

Lady Barrentine had already hurried away when Lillian met him at the bottom of the stairs.

"Good morning," he said, a shy look in his eyes that went away after she smiled and replied in kind.

"Would you take a ride with me? I am happy to take Bella with us, but Mother said she and Emma would look after her—"

"Yes, I would." She let out a breath, making her realize how much she'd wanted to spend some time alone with him before the wedding. "I will change and be back down in a few minutes."

He nodded.

Even with Bella asleep on her bed, and with Lillian trying to not wake her, she changed into her riding clothes and was downstairs within minutes to find Nash waiting for her.

As they went out to the stable, she glanced at him from the corner of her eye. It was so strange that she would be marrying this man the very next day. At times the thought of marrying him was exciting, but at this moment, it filled her with fear.

"I thought you might want to see more of the estate," he said, "and I thought I would show you some of my favorite places."

"Thank you. That sounds lovely."

They were still so awkward around each other. But they would be husband and wife tomorrow—unless she changed her mind.

She couldn't help remembering how excited she'd been before her first wedding, how full of hope she was at the thought of marrying into the Courtney family. She thought her husband's mother possessed a strong personality, but she never had an inkling how controlling she was. She had no idea that her husband would treat her badly, would ignore her, lash out at her for no reason, drink himself into a stupor so many times, and hit her in the back, not once but twice.

What was in store for her in this, her second marriage, about which she had no inkling? Was she taking Bella into something she would later regret?

Their horses were already saddled and ready for them. Instead of trusting the groom to help her, Nash himself bent and let her place her foot in his hand and boosted her up into the saddle. Then he mounted his own horse and they set out at a walk.

"I don't want to bore you," he said, "by telling you my grandfather planted this or that stand of trees, or who is farming which fields. Of course, you may ask anything you wish. But I particularly wanted to show you the small house my great-grandfather lived in while he was renovating and building onto Dunbridge Hall many years ago."

"That sounds very pleasant." Lillian pointed out a large nest at the top of a tree.

"A pair of storks have built and rebuilt that nest every year for the past several years."

"You must go on a lot of rides."

"Yes. When I'm writing a story, if I can't think of what should come next, sometimes I go for a walk or a ride and the story starts to unfold in my mind."

"That is interesting. Before I married, I sometimes wrote music, for the pianoforte. Once, I went for a walk and heard a bird singing, and suddenly I could hear the rest of the song I'd been writing. It was as if the bird made me remember what was in my head."

He smiled. "I would be very pleased to hear some of your music, songs that you wrote."

"That was a long time ago. I would have to search for them, as I don't remember them anymore."

They rode on, and Lillian admired the wildflowers growing along the edge of the trail and around the edges of the fields. Her senses were flooded with the beauty of bright red poppies, blue chicory, the purple of the corn-cockles and ragged robin, white daisies, bright yellow buttercups, and the pale pink of the pink thrift and milk-maid, which resembled a lovely low-lying fog where it grew thick in one particular meadow.

"Is the weather too warm for you? We could take a shadier path," he offered.

"I like the sun on my face." It felt strangely familiar and intimate to say such things, especially since ladies weren't supposed to allow the sun to freckle their faces. It felt good to say just what she was thinking and feeling to this man.

In fact, she suddenly realized that she was testing him by saying that, to see if he would behave as her first husband had. Her first husband had never tried to make conversation with her and rarely replied to anything she said, especially when she said something unexpected or out of the ordinary.

Nash just smiled. "I like the sun too. Perhaps we were born in the wrong country, do you think?"

"Yes, perhaps." Lillian grinned back. "But I think I would miss foggy, drizzily England, if I were to live some-where like Egypt, or on an island near the equator."

"What would you miss?"

"I'd miss our oak trees—all our trees—and our wildflowers. And there is something comforting about lying in bed, or sitting next to the fire, reading a good book while it rains outside the window. I'd miss rain if it was sunny every day."

He said quietly, "Perhaps it's the rain that makes us enjoy the sunshine."

As they rode along at an easy pace, she remembered what she'd been wondering ever since she agreed to marry him, and that was . . . What would Nash Golding, the Earl of Barrentine, do when he was angry? How would he behave when she did something he didn't like?

As before, when she'd tested him to see how he would react to her saying something out of the ordinary, she wanted to test him again, to discover what sort of temper he had. But when she thought about it as testing him, it seemed wrong somehow. And yet she had only one day to find out . . . before it was too late to back out of marrying him.

She'd seen how brave and noble he could be when he'd saved her from the man who attacked her in the village of Gantt. Afterward, he'd been comforting in his calm manner and attentiveness toward her. That proved something of his character, that he was a better man than her first husband, did it not?

They arrived at an old cottage in the woods, overgrown with vines and small trees, the thatch roof looking more like a nest for all the rodents thereabouts than a roof.

"This is where my great-grandparents stayed while they waited for the work on Dunbridge Hall to be finished, or at least for a part of it to be livable. I've always thought it a rather romantic spot, with the woods all around it. And there's a small spring behind it, which was their source of clean water. Would you like to see it?"

"Yes, I would. I love to imagine what old places were like when they were new, the people who lived there."

They moved their horses closer to the house, and Nash dismounted. "I will help you dismount if you like, as there are a lot of low-hanging branches."

He approached and Lillian unhooked her leg from the sidesaddle. She placed her hands on his shoulders and let her eyes meet his as he gazed up at her. And once more, she reminded herself, *We'll be married tomorrow.*

He was handsome, and he was closer to her own age than her first husband was. Indeed, everything about him appealed to her—partially because his appearance was so opposite Mr. Courtney's. He was taller, his build broader, even his hands were noticeably bigger. His eyes were bluer, his lips fuller.

Now her heart was beating rapidly, her breath becoming shallow, as she stared at him and imagined . . . What would it be like to kiss him? Would she enjoy it more than she'd enjoyed . . . But she shouldn't be thinking such thoughts. It felt crass and she even felt a bit of guilt, as if she was betraying her first husband. And maybe even her second one too.

His hands on either side of her waist were gentle but firm as he easily lifted her and slowly placed her feet on the ground.

"Thank you," she said, as he continued to hold her gaze. And the way he was looking at her, still holding onto her waist, she felt more loved than she had her whole marriage.

That was a strange thought. But she couldn't deny the pleasant warmth spreading through her.

His horse took a few steps away from them, and

Nash finally broke her gaze to go after him. Then, with each of them taking hold of the reins of their steeds, Nash came back to her and took her hand in his. They walked together into the woods.

Why should holding Nash's hand make her heart race so fast? She was being foolish. Besides, they would be married soon and then she surely wouldn't be this excited by a simple touch of his hand.

As they made their way toward the bottom of a small hill, she gradually began to be aware of a pleasant sound of trickling water.

Flowers grew all around the spring, different varieties than they'd seen beside the road and the fields. These flowers flourished in this wetter place with less sunlight, but they were no less beautiful.

Nash let go of her hand and pointed to the ground. "There's the spring head."

Her hand felt bereft, but Nash stayed close to her side as she admired the scenery. She wanted to remember this moment forever, the way it felt to be the center of Nash's attention.

CHAPTER SIXTEEN

Nash wasn't sure why he'd taken her hand. It had been impulsive, but Lillian didn't seem to mind, and she held his hand with equal pressure.

He marveled at how soft her skin was and how delicate her small hand felt inside his. But he didn't want to make her uncomfortable, so he released her hand when they reached the spring.

"I love the wildness of it," she said, looking all around her, her eyes wide. "It's as if we're in a place that has been untouched by man for hundreds of years."

"It is rather refreshing to see nature without man's influence and presence."

"Exactly. No trees planted in straight lines or rows of hedges. Everything is perfectly haphazard and natural."

Her interest and obvious admiration for the place made his chest expand. It shouldn't matter so much, perhaps, but it did please him that she enjoyed coming here. She was no simpering waif who couldn't admire nature enough to leave the sitting room.

Something caught Nash's eye. He took a few steps closer to the trickling water that seemed to appear by magic out of the soggy ground, and bent to stare at what looked like a footprint.

"Perhaps it's not as untouched by man as we thought," he said, and pointed it out to Lillian.

She drew nearer, though not close enough to sink into the mud. "A footprint. Could it have been one of your tenants?"

"Yes, it could." He lifted his head and straightened, staring all around with narrowed eyes, remembering what the groom had told him of seeing a man skulking about.

He started back toward the house. He felt his shoulder tense and his mind went to the pistol he kept in his saddlebag.

"Is everything all right?"

"Probably. But I want to make sure no one is in the house."

He approached the structure cautiously, and Lillian stayed behind him, as they each led their horses by their reins.

Nash went to the door and pushed it open with a creaking sound. He opened the shutters on the front side of the house, all the while listening for any unusual sounds.

"I'll only be a moment," he told her, glancing around once more to make sure she was safe to be left outside. Then he went into the house.

There was just enough light through the open windows to be able to see that someone had been inside the front room, and there was even what looked like a makeshift bed on the floor—blankets and a pillow piled against the wall.

Nash looked out the window. Lillian was still there, standing with the horses.

He was conflicted as to what to do. Should he take Lillian home and come back with more men to search the house? By then the man would surely be gone. But if this was the man who accosted Lillian in Gantt, he was obviously bent on harming her, and Nash needed to apprehend him—now.

Nash looked around the front room, but seeing no clues as to the man's identity, he went back out to get his gun.

"Is someone inside?" she asked, her eyes widening when she saw him pull out his pistol.

"Probably not, but I want to make sure. I can take you back to the main house first, if you prefer."

"No, I'll be all right here."

"Scream if you see or hear anyone."

"I will."

She looked quite brave standing there with the reins in her hand.

"Then again, I think you should be ready to ride in case something goes badly." He stuck the gun in his waistband and went to her, bending down and linking his fingers. She placed her foot in his makeshift stirrup and he boosted her into the saddle.

"Ride away if you hear a gunshot, or if anything else happens."

She nodded, a glint of bravery coupled with defiance in her eyes.

But nothing would happen.

He went inside and looked through all the rooms on the bottom floor. It was obvious someone had been building fires in the fireplaces and living there, even preparing food. He climbed the stairs but found nothing suspicious. When he was satisfied no one was there—constantly checking out the window to make sure Lillian was safe—he went back down the stairs and outside to join her.

"He is gone. But someone has been here."

"Perhaps it is only a wanderer who stayed for a while and left."

"Perhaps."

"But I can see you don't believe that. Who do you think it is?"

She was sharp, the kind of intelligence women often pretended not to possess. Perhaps he should tell her the truth.

"I am still seeking the man who attacked you in the village near Stokemont Abbey. And one of my grooms saw a man skulking about near the stables a week ago. It may not be the same man, but it may be. The evidence is starting to accumulate that someone with evil intentions is still stalking you."

And that made Nash angry. No one had the right to stalk and harm any natural-born subject of the English Crown, or any other innocent person, for that matter, but this woman was his wife-to-be. Not only that, but he knew her to be innocent—or at least, he believed her to be.

"But why would anyone want to harm me? It makes no sense." But even as she said the words, a hint of realization seemed to flicker across her face, changing her expression.

"You know Mrs. Courtney perhaps better than anyone. Do you think she would have you killed in order to take over guardianship of Bella?"

"Because of what Mrs. Courtney said after the constable left, I did have an idea that she might have hired that man in the village to frighten me—not to kill me or even to harm me, but just to frighten me—so that I would stay at Stokemont Abbey out of fear and a desire for protection. But would she have me killed? I don't know. I honestly don't know."

The fact that Lillian didn't come to the woman's defense told him that yes, Mrs. Courtney probably was capable of having her killed.

They were still in the small clearing in front of "the old house near the spring," as they called it. But he suddenly felt the need to get Lillian back to Dunbridge Hall.

He stuffed his pistol, which he'd been pointing at the ground, into the waistband of his pants and nodded to her. "I think we'd better—"

A shot rang out.

Nash snatched the pistol out and pointed it in the direction where he thought he'd heard the shot.

"Ride!" he shouted at Lillian. Then he sprang onto his horse and rode hard toward the woods.

He saw a streak of brown through the trees as the shooter was obviously on a horse as well, but he was well ahead of him.

Not wanting to waste any bullets or betray his own location, Nash resisted the urge to shoot a round in the direction he'd glimpsed him.

He realized he hadn't even looked to see if Lillian was all right. What if she was shot?

He felt sick at the thought, but he pursued the shooter until he realized he had no idea where he had gone. He found the road that led back to Dunbridge Hall, but there was no sign of recent hoofprints, especially a horse at a fast gallop. He looked around for a few minutes, but seeing no evidence of the man, he rode hard back toward where he had left Lillian.

When he reached the clearing, there was no sign of her. "Lillian!" he called.

Had she ridden back to Dunbridge Hall? Was the shooter circling back to find her?

His heart was in his throat as he rode toward home.

CHAPTER SEVENTEEN

Lillian stopped her horse and looked all around her. She was lost.

She stayed in the woods, fearful of being seen by the shooter if she ventured onto the road, but she couldn't go very fast among the trees. And she also had no idea which direction she was going.

The sun, which had been so warm a short while before, was now hidden behind the clouds. It might have offered her clues to which direction she had gone, but there was no sign of it in the clouds overhead—when the leaves of the thick forest allowed her to see the sky.

She'd once been told by her brother that lichens and moss usually grew only on the north side of trees, so she started looking for them. Her heart was still thumping wildly after the terror of being shot at. *O God, please don't let Nash be hurt.*

She found them, but they were not all growing on the same side of every tree. But it was consistent enough that she eventually decided on which way was north.

When they'd set out from Dunbridge Hall, they'd

been going in a south, southwest direction. So she turned her horse toward what she thought was north and urged her forward.

Gradually, she became aware of a trickling sensation on her upper arm. Was a spider crawling down her arm under the sleeve of her riding clothes? But then she felt a breath of cool air on her upper arm and shoulder. Turning her head to see, she touched her arm and her fingers came away covered with bright red blood.

Her sleeve was torn and her arm was bleeding. Only then did she feel pain, but it was the pain of a scratch, not how she would imagine a bullet wound would feel. Had a limb scraped her hard enough to tear her sleeve?

She continued to ride, still very unsure where she was going, when she heard a faint sound. She stopped her horse to listen. Someone was calling her name, and the voice sounded like Nash.

"I'm here!" she yelled back, but it was a weak yell. She tried again, louder this time.

Soon, she could hear horse's hooves crashing through the underbrush.

"Keep calling!" the voice said.

"I'm here!" she called again, now moving in his direction.

Finally, she caught sight of him and her hands started shaking. By the time he reached her, he was dismounting from his horse and reaching for her, his eyes focused on her arm.

"He shot you."

She was out of her saddle in moments and in his arms, burying her face in his cravat. One of his arms was around her, as strong as a steel band, while his other hand was pulling at her torn sleeve.

"You're hurt. I will kill the man."

She was trembling from head to toe at the thought of someone shooting her. But he was so solid and warm, and she'd never felt so protected. *O God, thank you for this man.*

"I am well," she whispered. "But I got lost."

He pulled away and looked into her face. "Are you all right?"

"Yes. It is only a scratch, I think." She tried to sound brave, not wanting him to realize how shaken she was. But she was loathe to leave his arms.

"Thank God," he breathed. "I will kill that man. I will find him and kill him for this."

She buried her face in his shoulder, hugging him tight.

"Come," he said. "We must get you home where you'll be safe. I intend to find this man, even if I have to send word to every man in the county to help me find him."

She reluctantly left his arms, not wishing to make things awkward, and still trying to make him think she was brave.

He helped her mount her horse, his eyes lingering on her face, her hand lingering on his shoulder.

She followed him, and realized she'd been going in the opposite direction from Dunbridge Hall. So much for finding the moss on the trees. But then again, she wasn't sure what direction she'd been going, or how far she'd gone, before she found the moss on the trees.

Nash rode with his pistol in one hand and the reins in the other, keeping quite close to her as they rode. When they reached a point where she recognized they were near

Dunbridge Hall, she still didn't let her guard down, and neither did Nash, by the tense way he held his shoulders and kept glancing around.

At the stable, Nash informed the grooms what had happened and gave them several orders, having them ready themselves to help search for the shooter, as well as informing their nearest neighbors and friends of the danger and the need to find this shooter before he managed to harm them.

She slipped her hand inside the crook of his arm, and he walked briskly, his pistol still at the ready, all the way to the house. Only then did she feel herself relax and let out the breath she'd been holding.

"Oh my! What is wrong?" Lady Barrentine came hurrying toward them.

"A man shot at us," Lillian said.

"He shot at Lillian and caught the edge of her arm with the bullet," Nash said, a hard edge in his voice.

"Oh, my dear!" Lady Barrentine exclaimed, closely examining Lillian's arm.

"I'm going to gather as many men as I can and search for him. I'm not sure when I'll be back. Please watch over Lillian, and neither one of you is to leave the house for any reason."

"Of course," Lady Barrentine said.

"Yes, of course," Lillian said.

Nash's eyes met hers in a long look that sent a tingling sensation to her toes. Then he strode from the house.

"I can hardly believe this happened right here at our own home," Lady Barrentine was lamenting. "And my poor Lillian! Thank God you are not more seriously hurt! I must get this bandaged and your clothes changed before sweet Bella sees you bleeding. Come, my dear."

As Lady Barrentine led her to the little sick room off the kitchen, Lillian's mind was full of Nash—the way he'd looked at her, the concern in his eyes, the anger toward the shooter. He may have been reacting as any landowner would in such circumstances, having a trespasser on his land who would dare shoot at him or a guest. But she so wanted to believe that his strong emotion meant that he did care for her, at least a little.

How desperately she longed for his love.

~ ~ ~

Heat pulsed through Nash's body, filling his forehead like liquid fury, when he thought about the man trying to kill Lillian right in front of him. How dare anyone shoot at his future wife, and in his very presence? He would find the man or die trying.

But what if the man had shot Lillian just a few bare inches to the left? He'd have hit her heart.

But he couldn't, wouldn't think about that now, except to allow it to fuel his anger and determination to find the man who did this.

He rode out with a small group that had already gathered, having heard the word. He'd also sent messages to all of his tenants, as well as all the landowners who lived nearby, along with the constable and the Justice of the Peace.

Besides his thoughts of capturing the fiend who'd tried to kill Lillian, his mind was full of Lillian herself— her soft skin, her lovely smile, her obvious bravery. Most of all, he remembered the way she'd dismounted before he could even help her down, the way she pressed herself to him, her arms wrapping tightly around him. He liked remembering how that felt, and he wanted more of that, feeling as if a beautiful woman was thankful for him and trusted and relied on him. She made him feel like he was the hero of one of those unrealistic novels he was always ridiculing.

He needed to rethink some things, but later, when he was not chasing a would-be killer.

~ ~ ~

Lillian and Lady Barrentine were both on edge, waiting to hear that Nash had arrived home. But night fell, and they found themselves dining with only Mildred and Emma, who were unusually quiet.

Lillian prayed silently, quick prayers begging God to keep Nash safe and bring him back unharmed. She wanted him to capture the shooter, but not if it meant he would be harmed.

Finally, in the middle of dinner, word came that Nash was home and was going up to his room to change and get cleaned up.

He joined them later in the drawing room looking tired and solemn.

"There was no sign of him anywhere," Nash said. At one point there were fifty men searching for him, but we found . . . nothing."

"Perhaps he will leave and never come back," Lady Barrentine said. "It is possible. He certainly knows you are looking for him. He will not dare to continue in this area. He is surely long gone by now."

"I wish I could think the same, but whoever he is, he seems determined to harm Lillian. I believe someone must be paying him. Lillian—" He leaned forward and captured her eyes with his. "Can you think of anyone, anyone at all, who might be holding a grudge against you and might want to kill you, for any reason?"

"Only Mrs. Courtney, and you know the reasons."

Bella was already in bed, being watched over by the servant who was Bella's favorite—and was fast becoming a candidate to replace her nurse—so Lillian didn't have to be careful what she said. Still, it felt wrong to elaborate, in case a servant was listening.

Nash lowered his voice. "I do believe she is the one who has hired this man to harm you."

"Could she have heard about the wedding?" Lady Barrentine whispered.

"I don't know how, since we have told no one," Lillian said.

"Once you are married, she must know that Nash will be made guardian of Bella," Lady Barrentine went on. "She may try to stop the wedding."

"She cannot stop the wedding," Nash said confidently. "It is tomorrow morning. But if she doesn't know about it, she will continue her plan."

"Then we must spread the news that you are wed," Lady Barrentine said.

Nash looked at Lillian.

"I have no reason to want to keep it a secret," Lillian said.

"Then I shall have it printed in the papers as soon as possible," Lady Barrentine said. "Then Mrs. Courtney shall have no further reason to wish to harm you."

"Unless," Nash said, "she thought that the courts would grant her guardianship of Bella if Lillian died soon after our wedding."

Lady Barrentine sighed, looking as if she agreed.

"I suppose I must stay alive, then." Lillian smiled, trying to lighten the mood, but neither her soon-to-be husband nor mother-in-law changed their sober expressions.

"Son, you look tired. Why don't you go to bed. Tomorrow is a very important day."

"Yes." Nash looked at Lillian. "I will see you both in the morning."

"I should go to bed too," Lillian said, hoping Nash would walk her to her door, but he was already on his way out.

Lillian had a niggling feeling in her chest that she should ask Nash to postpone the wedding. But she'd given her word to marry him. Everything was already planned and ready. Tomorrow she would be married to the Earl of Barrentine and Bella would be safe from Mrs. Courtney. Everything would work out well. So why did her heart feel so hollow?

CHAPTER EIGHTEEN

Nash awoke the next morning still unsure what to do. He had asked Lillian to marry him partially as a way of protecting her and Bella from Mrs. Courtney's schemes. They had not known each other long, hardly long enough to form an attachment. Part of him said that the thoughtful thing to do would be to allow Lillian to spend their first night of marriage without him. To do otherwise did not seem chivalrous. But part of him very much wished to spend their first night together.

He got out of bed and hurried to get clean, dressed, and ready for his wedding, which would take place that very morning. And besides the wedding, at any moment he might receive word saying someone had captured the man who shot at Lillian, or that he'd been seen, or that he was cornered and was being held at bay. Surely the man could not get away, with so many people searching for him.

As he got ready, he did get a few messages from his tenants, friends, and his grooms who had all been searching for the shooter, but none of them had found anything helpful.

"We need men to accompany us to the church," he told his manservant.

"I shall make sure of it, sir," he said.

With several men as guards on horseback, Nash rode in the carriage to the church with Mildred, Emma, his mother, Lillian, and Bella, and he was glad it was a short way, for although Bella was entertaining them all with her smiles and giggles, as she was in an especially happy mood, Mildred's stare was almost a glare. Her disapproval made him wish it were acceptable to tell his sister she was a daft little brat.

Truthfully, reason warned him that he might be making a mistake—which made her disapproval all the more annoying. But whenever he looked at Lillian, his emotions told him he was doing the right thing, and that he would not regret marrying her.

And that was just the sort of thing he might read in one of the popular novels that he satirized.

Lillian, who sat beside him, with Bella crawling from her lap to his and back again, whispered, "I'm sorry Bella is so full of high spirits today."

"It is not a problem. I like seeing her happy."

They smiled at each other, and once again, he felt his own spirits rise.

Bella suddenly stood in Nash's lap and looked him in the eye. She pressed her little palm to his cheek, then took his hand and pressed it to her own cheek. "Papa," she said softly.

Nash's heart did a crazy somersault and he smiled at her. "Bella's Papa," he whispered back. No one heard him but Bella, as the women were talking of weddings and wedding dresses and where he and Lillian might travel on their wedding trip, and how they could not go anywhere until the shooter was caught.

Bella put both her hands on his face and leaned forward and kissed him on the cheek.

"Aw, Bella," Emma said. "Mother, did you see that? Bella just kissed Nash on the cheek."

While Mother and Emma were cooing over Bella, he looked at Lillian and she was blinking back tears. She reached over and squeezed his arm, but immediately had to let go, as the child jumped into her lap, giggling and hiding her face in Lillian's chest.

Yes, everything would be well.

~ ~ ~

If Lillian's first wedding had seemed to happen in slow motion, this one seemed to happen in double time. Before she could put two thoughts together, the rector was declaring them "man and wife."

Nash was a good man, and she was also doing this for Bella. But she hated that everyone would say she was a mercenary, only marrying Nash for her own status and worldly gain and not for love.

Perhaps in the beginning, they would have been right.

She had become quite fond of Nash in the last few weeks. How could she not? He was kind and considerate and courageous, and she found him more handsome with every passing day. And she had even decided she was in love with him. At least she would know what it was like to have a mother-in-law who didn't hate her, but was kind to her.

Once they were outside in the churchyard, Lillian could see just how small was the crowd that had come to their wedding. Her brother Christopher had not come.

She'd sent an invitation to him and Gretchen, though it had been short notice. And since Nash's married sister had not attended, there was only Lady Barrentine, Mildred, Emma, Bella, and a neighbor who was a friend of Nash's, a Mr. Robert Kincaid.

Bella was reaching for Lillian, so she was just taking her from Emma's arms when she glanced up and noticed a woman about thirty yards away, slowly walking toward them. She seemed to be concealing something behind her, amongst her skirts.

Nash must have noticed her at the same time, for he pointed her out to one of the footmen, who stood nearby. He then turned to Mr. Kincaid, his friend. "Do you know that woman?"

He squinted and shook his head. "Never seen her before."

She kept walking toward him, and when she was about twenty yards away, she raised her arm and pointed a long-barreled pistol at them.

A few shouts rang out just before the spark of the flintlock hammer and the loud crack of the shot.

Lillian dropped to her knees, still holding Bella, shielding her with her body.

There were a few screams, while Bella wriggled in her arms, trying to see over her shoulder.

Lillian turned her head to see Nash, his friend Kincaid, and two footmen running after the fleeing woman. They seized her and took the gun from her hands.

"Are you and Bella hurt?" Lady Barrentine asked, helping Lillian and Bella up.

"No. Is Nash all right?" She couldn't be sure, but she'd thought the woman had aimed the gun at him.

"I don't think he was hurt." Lady Barrentine turned

her attention to the chaos twenty yards away, where the men were holding the woman by her arms and shoulders.

"Nash!" Lady Barrentine called out. "Are you hurt?"

Nash shook his head and looked back at them. "Is everyone all right there?"

"We are well."

The clergyman had come out of the church and was frantically asking what had happened. Mildred was trying to explain, while Emma was clutched at her chest and saying, "That was the most exciting thing that's ever happened at a wedding, I daresay."

"Who is that woman?" Lady Barrentine asked, glancing at Lillian.

"I've never seen her before."

The woman was shouting at Nash. Since they now seemed safe, as Mr. Kincaid was holding the woman's pistol, Lillian went closer to hear what the woman was saying.

"How dare you ridicule Mrs. Radcliffe! Mrs. Radcliffe is better than two of you!" the woman was screaming.

"Have you been sleeping in the cottage in the woods, the one beside the spring?"

"What if I have?" the woman yelled.

"Did you shoot at my wife and me yesterday?"

"I was not shooting at her. I was shooting at you!" She suddenly threw herself at him, breaking free from the men who had been holding onto her.

She scratched at him like a feral cat, just before the men grabbed hold of her and pulled her off of him.

"What did Lord Barrentine do to you?" Mr. Kincaid demanded of the woman.

"He is trying to ruin Mrs. Radcliffe! How dare he

criticize her work? Shame on you!" she screamed, her face as red as fire. "For shame!"

Nash took several steps back, away from the distraught woman who was still struggling against her captors, tears running down her red cheeks.

When Bella, who was clinging to Lillian's neck, saw Nash, she started to cry.

"It's all right. Everything's all right, Bella," he said, but he looked rather pale.

"You have blood on your neck," Lillian said.

He took a handkerchief from his pocket and dabbed at the bloody scratch. "Why don't you take Bella back home. We will send word to the constable and Justice of the Peace and . . ." He looked her in the eye and said softly, "I'm sorry."

"You are not to blame," Lillian said, as they both walked away from the woman, who was still screaming. "The woman is obviously deranged."

But the expression on Nash's face told her he was not sure about that, that the woman's words had shaken him.

"At least now you are safe," he said.

They approached his mother, and he said, "Take everyone back to Dunbridge Hall. All is well now. There is no more danger." But by the tone of his voice, one would have thought he was announcing the death of a close friend or relative.

"That horrible woman," Lady Barrentine said. "How dare she shoot at you and accuse you? Can she love Mrs. Radcliffe that much? You never ridiculed that woman at all."

"Only her novels," Nash said. "Go on home. I'll be there as soon as I can."

Without a glance at Lillian, he turned and began giving orders to the men who had come to help provide protection, servants and friends who had stood guard outside the church during the wedding. Now they'd be sent for the constable and other authorities.

Without a doubt, this must be one of the strangest wedding days ever. Lillian felt let down, her stomach and her heart both sinking to her toes, as she and Bella rode home without her new husband.

CHAPTER NINETEEN

The servants were waiting to congratulate them when they arrived home, but Lillian could see the confusion on their faces when they saw them exit the carriage without the master of the house.

"All is well," Lady Barrentine told them. "The wedding was beautiful and Lord Barrentine will be along shortly."

But Lillian felt her cheeks flush, as she was stared at and wondered about, arriving without the man she had just married.

Inside, the wedding breakfast was laid out in the dining room, buffet style. But rather than a festive occasion, the atmosphere was subdued, and Bella promptly fell asleep in Lillian's lap.

"Lillian, let Sukey take Bella to her bed."

Sukey was standing by and came forward, gently extracting Bella's limp form from Lillian's arms. When Bella began to stir, Sukey said in a soft voice, "That's my good girl," and Bella's eyes closed again as she laid her head on the young servant's shoulder.

Lillian tried to join in the conversation, trying not to betray her state of mind, but she could barely force down two bites of food.

Now that Nash knew that neither Mrs. Courtney nor anyone else was trying to kill Lillian, would he regret marrying her? But he had been marrying her so that Bella would not be taken away. And the way he had barely even looked at Lillian after the wedding, she began to wonder if theirs would ever be a marriage of love. Perhaps it would always be just a marriage of convenience.

But she was mired in gloom again. Why did her thoughts always go to the worst thing that could happen?

Two hours went by. Even Lady Barrentine sat listlessly staring out the window, while Mildred and Emma played a rhyming game at the far end of the table, trading words almost as boys might trade fencing strikes.

A sound was heard down the hall, like the back door opening and closing. Lady Barrentine sat up straight and Lillian nervously brushed the front of her gown and patted her hair.

"You look beautiful," Lady Barrentine said.

A few moments later, Nash and Mr. Kincaid entered the room and bowed to them.

"Forgive our tardiness," Mr. Kincaid said when Nash did not speak.

"Did the constable take the deranged woman to jail?" Lady Barrentine asked.

"She is locked away where she cannot harm anyone," Mr. Kincaid said, starting to smile. "My friend here has made quite the enemy."

Nash took a deep breath and let it out.

"Don't worry, my dear," Lady Barrentine. "All of this silliness and controversy over your books will die down and be forgotten in no time. There will always be those whose minds have become unhinged, and I shouldn't wonder, if they are reading those novels by Mrs. Radcliffe. Hannah More is a very popular writer and she greatly disapproves of Mrs. Radcliffe's novels, you know, and she is of a very steady and religious mind."

"Yes, Mother. Let us not talk of it."

Nash looked at Lillian. "Are you well? Was Bella upset?"

"Bella forgot all about it as soon as we were in the carriage. She's asleep—oh, no, there she is."

Sukey walked in with Bella, as if on cue. Bella was already reaching for Lillian.

The scratch on Nash's neck had been cleaned up and, though red, it did not look as bad as before. Now, as Mr. Kincaid made pleasant conversation with Nash's mother and sisters, Nash came to sit close beside her.

"Do take some food. You must be famished."

"I should be, but I don't feel it." Nevertheless, he put some food on his plate and took a bite.

She watched him eat and said a quick prayer that all might yet be well.

~ ~ ~

Nash was not very hungry, but he didn't want anyone to know how dark his thoughts were. So, he choked down a few bites of the feast that had been prepared for the wedding party.

When he'd got out of bed that morning, he'd hoped to look back on this day as a happy one, a day when he'd taken a step of faith that turned out to be the best decision he'd ever made. Instead, he would look back on this day as a day he, or indeed, anyone at the wedding today, could have been killed by a deranged woman who took issue with the novels he'd written and published. He was still trying to get her words out of his head. "Shame on you! For shame!"

And it was true. He'd done something shameful by attacking a woman's work, another man's wife, Mrs. Radcliffe. He'd hidden behind anonymity, and now that was torn away and the readers who loved Mrs. Radcliffe's novels . . . hated him. And he could hardly blame them. It was very unchivalrous of him, to say the least.

The last few times he'd sat down to write, he'd felt like a rogue and a villain. What was he doing, ridiculing another writer's work? After all, it was much easier to criticize than it was to create. He'd created his own stories, but the purpose had been to show how ridiculous Mrs. Radcliffe's were, how they intentionally manipulated the emotions and created fear in her readers.

But what right did he have to criticize? He knew how it felt, every time he read a scathing review of his own novels—which, admittedly, were few, as he had only a fraction of Mrs. Radcliffe's readers.

These were the thoughts that had gone around and around in his head for the past two hours, while his new wife and most of his family sat celebrating—or trying to celebrate—his marriage to this beautiful, longsuffering woman.

He drank the rest of his wine and turned to Lillian. "Forgive me for leaving you alone after the wedding. I am sure you must be . . ." What could he even say? That she must be sorry she'd married him? A man who was not only a laughingstock but also an unchivalrous scoundrel, a man who criticized and ridiculed those who were conscientiously engaged in the same work that he was.

"I am well, I assure you." Lillian smiled.

"She scratched you," Bella said, reaching a tiny hand out to pat his cheek. "Like a cat!" Bella bared her teeth and curved her fingers like claws.

Nash couldn't help but smile and shake his head, though a bit ruefully. "She did, didn't she, Bella?"

"A cat scratched me. I don't like that cat. He scratched me on my hand." She pointed to the long-healed spot on her hand.

"That was a naughty cat," Nash said, "to scratch my Bella."

Bella giggled, a joyful sound that cheered even him.

When Bella's melodic laugh finally quieted, she said, "I don't have any claws." She examined her fingers as if to make sure.

"Because you are a lovely little lady."

Bella laughed again, the high-pitched sound ending as abruptly as it started. "I'm not a lady. I'm a girl. And you are Mamma's husband."

"That is right, Bella."

He had wondered if she'd even understood what was happening, but she probably understood more than anyone gave her credit for.

To Bella, he wasn't a disgraced earl who wrote foolish novels that very few people would enjoy, or a wealthy man to be envied, or even a Member of Parliament who was too afraid of saying something foolish to say anything at all. No, to Bella he was her mother's new husband, and if he treated her as he should, she'd one day see him as her Papa, hopefully forgetting she'd ever had another.

Bella's attention was suddenly arrested by Lady Barrentine pointing out that Cook had made Bella's favorite cake.

"Thank you for being so patient with Bella." Lillian was gazing at him with those liquid blue eyes of hers.

"She is easy to love, a little cherub of plump cheeks and wise words."

"Wise words?" Lillian smiled in amusement as Bella climbed out of her lap and into Lady Barrentine's to be closer to the cake and candied fruit.

"For a three-year-old, you must admit, she is very wise."

Lillian laughed, and the sound, though much quieter, revived him just as much as Bella's.

"I know she likes you very much."

"I hope I won't disappoint her."

"You won't."

"How do you know?"

Lillian gazed at him a long moment before speaking. "The fact that you even care about disappointing her means you won't."

He wanted to kiss her, but he didn't want to make her uncomfortable. Besides that, he was well aware of his mother, sisters, and friend in the same room.

They were staring into each other's eyes when he heard his sister Emma say, "Nash, have you even kissed your bride yet? Kiss her."

He wasn't sure what to say, but he could see Lillian's cheeks turning red.

"You're making Lady Barrentine uncomfortable."

Lillian glanced at his mother, as if she didn't realize he was talking about her. "You are Lady Barrentine now," he whispered.

She blushed even more and ducked her head.

"Kiss her," Emma said again.

"Unless it's not that kind of marriage," Mildred

murmured.

A hush fell on the room.

"Mildred." Mother's tone was scolding. "Hold your tongue, miss."

But Mildred did not look sorry.

"You can kiss me," Lillian said—then, even more quietly, "I don't mind."

He stared into her eyes until her gaze fell to his lips.

His heart thrummed in his chest. He leaned down and pressed his lips to hers, feeling the way she kissed him back—barely anything at all, but enough that he felt her interest.

Even with all the people watching them, he didn't want to end the kiss. But she ended it for him, ducking her head shyly.

No one there knew—although they probably all suspected—that was his first kiss.

Certainly, if she hadn't already, Lillian would soon recognize his complete inexperience.

Kincaid, as well as his sisters and mother, were all showing their approval. Lillian was obviously embarrassed, but she smiled good-naturedly.

Lillian nibbled nervously on a bit of cake, and Nash got himself another glass of wine.

He shouldn't be embarrassed by his lack of experience. Besides, he was well aware that Lillian's primary reason for marrying him was to keep Bella with her. Perhaps she would not be in any hurry to find out how inexperienced he was.

That thought sank in like a load of bricks.

At least she had not minded kissing him, even in front of his family.

His mood was greatly deflated by the woman

whose great love for Mrs. Radcliffe and her novels had driven her to try to kill him. Yes, as Kincaid had told him more than once in the last two hours, the woman was obviously mad. Still, he felt as if he had nothing to be proud of in his own novels. Even though people had said his books made them laugh, they were essentially laughing at Mrs. Radcliffe and the other popular authors of the day.

He needed to stop thinking about this. He pushed the gloomy thoughts away and turned his attention on the conversation around him.

Emma was complimenting Lillian's dress and hair. "I do believe you were the prettiest bride I've ever seen."

"You are too kind," Lillian protested with a shake of her head. "But I thank you."

"Mamma is the prettiest mamma," Bella chimed in, kissing her mother's cheek.

Nash's heart squeezed in his chest. How could he not fall in love with such a loving mother as Lillian? And he must win her love in return, must make her forget that he'd almost gotten her killed at their wedding, and make her forget that she agreed to marry him out of necessity and the love of her child, rather than her love for him.

"What we need is some jolly music to celebrate Nash and Lillian's wedding," Emma called out. "Mother, may we retire to the music room?"

They all seemed in agreement, and soon Mildred was playing a lively tune and Mr. Kincaid was asking Emma to dance.

Nash looked at Lillian. "Will you dance with me?"

"Yes, Mamma!" Bella said with a gleeful smile. "Dance! Dance!"

Lillian's smile was intoxicating as she placed her hand in his and let him lead her to where Kincaid and

Emma had moved some chairs out of the way to create a small dance floor.

It was a lively dance, so he was only touching her hand at intervals, but all of her attention was on him, and it was going to straight to his head like a big glass of brandy. For the moment, she wasn't Bella's mother, she wasn't Courtney's widow, and she wasn't his mother's friend; she was his wife, and she seemed pleased to be.

When they briefly switched partners, and Nash found himself holding his sister Emma's hand, she winked at him, a sly look on her face.

Probably everyone in the room could see his infatuation written on his face. Well, he was not ashamed of it. He'd always intended to love his wife above all others.

When the music stopped, Mildred began to play something slower. Nash was glad, until he began to notice how Kincaid was looking at his sister, as well as how close they were as they danced. Was there something between his sister and his friend?

He liked Kincaid. He was a good sort, but Nash wasn't sure he was good enough for his youngest sister.

He'd have a word with him later. But this was his wedding day, and he wanted to put his attention on Lillian.

CHAPTER TWENTY

Lillian's heart skipped a few beats at the way Nash was looking at her. The touch of his hand as they danced, the blue of his eyes, his expression, all seemed to work together to heighten her awareness and send a longing through her that took her breath away. She felt as if she'd never lived before this moment.

She was Nash's wife now, and she wanted to forget she had ever been married before.

Bella was the daughter she loved, but she could imagine Bella had come to her straight from God, not from her first husband.

These were strange thoughts, but it was strange to be married again, and to someone with whom she was barely even acquainted a month ago.

Was one month too soon to fall in love?

Engagements had occurred upon much less acquaintance, and many marriages occurred without even a pretense of attachment. Many women married for a comfortable home and situation without ever forming an attachment to their husband. But such a thing was abhorrent to Lillian. She had always wanted to marry for love, and she'd married Mr. Courtney because she thought she loved him.

Perhaps it was better to marry someone of noble character, and then love would come, naturally.

Now that they were dancing a slower dance, a closer, more intimate dance, Nash seemed distracted. He kept glancing over at Emma and Mr. Kincaid. Was he afraid they were forming an attachment? Did he disapprove?

Her heart sank a bit, but then he turned his attention back on her.

"I'm sorry the day was not as we might have hoped. No woman wants to see her wedding day ruined by a crazed woman shooting at the wedding party."

"That was hardly your fault, so there is no need to apologize."

"One could argue that it was my fault. The woman was mad because of what I had done."

"Still, you are not to blame that she shot at us, and I would staunchly argue that you are not responsible for her deranged state of mind."

"How is your arm?"

"It does not even hurt."

"Many women would have become hysterical at being shot, but you bore it with complete equanimity."

"It was merely a scratch," she protested with a smile. "And perhaps I was more afraid than I let on." She raised her brows at him.

"You hid it well. And as for being shot at, twice, Mildred told me that if I was her husband-to-be, and if I was the cause of her being shot—she told me this after the woman was captured—she would have the marriage annulled and would never speak to me again."

Lillian laughed.

"Ah, you think that is amusing. Well, it is not often that we can laugh with amusement at what Mildred says." He was smiling good-naturedly.

The song ended and another began. In fact, they danced five dances together, until Mildred stopped playing. Then they all went back into the dining room and ate and drank some more.

Sukey had put Bella down for a nap and she'd awakened again, and Lillian was having to stifle a yawn. The day had taken a lot of energy out of her, and she was beginning to wish Mr. Kincaid would go home and she could go up to her room to rest, when a servant came in and whispered something in Nash's ear.

The servant left, and everyone stopped their conversations and looked to Nash.

"I'm afraid I must go. The Justice of the Peace has summoned me." He turned to Lillian and discreetly squeezed her hand. "I shall return as soon as I can."

"Of course."

Later, after Mr. Kincaid had taken his leave of them, Lillian asked Lady Barrentine, "How far away is the Justice of the Peace?"

Lady Barrentine looked sad. "It is at least a two-hour ride from here. I highly doubt he will be able to make it home by dinner."

And sure enough, they dined without him. His sisters talked about the latest fashions, their London outings, various friends, and Lady Barrentine seemed to talk quickly and with fervor, as if she was trying to distract Lillian from thinking about Nash not being there.

Lillian finally felt free to excuse herself after dinner

and went up to her room.

Her body felt exhausted, as if she'd been traveling all day, but her mind wouldn't let her sleep. Nash could come home at any moment. Would he knock on her door? It was their wedding night, after all. Or would he spend the night elsewhere, too tired to make it home? She remembered how he'd looked at her when they danced, and the longing she'd felt then came back threefold.

She lay awake, her mind in a whirl, her body tired but restless.

~ ~ ~

The Justice of the Peace was affable enough, but Nash couldn't shake the feeling that the JP blamed him, at least to a small extent, and did not approve of him or his novels. But perhaps he was projecting his own feelings onto the JP.

Nash answered the man's many questions, then listened to what he had to say of the woman who had shot at them twice.

"Her name is Letitia Morgan, and she was born illegitimately. Her mother is the daughter of a solicitor, and her father is the baronet Sir Begley, both of whom are deceased. Her aunt has given me permission to start the process of having her committed to an institution for the insane. She claims she is not dangerous to anyone except you, Lord Barrentine, but the fact is that she shot your wife, did she not?"

"The bullet only grazed her arm, I am thankful to Providence."

"That is a mercy. She is very fortunate, for you certainly know it could have been much worse."

"Yes, of course."

"I am recommending she be committed, but it is up

to the judge to decide, of course, unless you wish to bring criminal charges against her on behalf of yourself and your wife, and then we can have her tried for attempted murder."

Nash thought for a moment, then shook his head. "That will not be necessary." As bad as an insane asylum was, he had heard enough stories to know that to be locked in prison was worse.

"I will never understand why ladies like Mrs. Radcliffe are permitted to write such stories. They only stir up ladies' sensibilities in unnatural and dangerous ways. My own wife and daughter read her books and stay up all night. No good can come from that, I tell you."

Nash wasn't sure how to respond. He actually saw nothing wrong with Mrs. Radcliffe's novels, particularly, or with ladies reading them. His own sisters read them, as did Lillian, and they had not suffered any ill effects that he could tell.

"My own clergyman condemns the reading of such novels," the JP went on, "as they stir up dissatisfaction with the life and lot of proper English wives and daughters."

Again, Nash was not at all sure he agreed with the man. A novel could not create dissatisfaction. The dissatisfaction must be within the person to begin with, for the novel could not stir up what was not already there.

Nash rode home in the dark, pondering the JP's words, as well as the fate of the woman who had wanted to kill him for insulting her favorite author. He also pondered his own novels. He still wanted to write, but writing a novel in order to satirize someone else's work no longer appealed to him.

He arrived home to find the house dark, as everyone must have retired to bed a bit early. He found some food in the kitchen and ate it quickly, then went up the stairs with a light tread.

He paused in front of Lillian's door. Was she already asleep? It had been a long, tiring day for her, no doubt. She certainly wouldn't want him to wake her.

He rubbed a hand over his jaw, feeling the stubble. She probably wasn't expecting him to come to her tonight. He didn't want to frighten her or put pressure on her in any way. After all, she married him in order to protect her daughter, not because they had formed an attachment.

But they had developed fond feelings for each other, had they not? Certainly he had. But he could not risk seeing her recoil from him in shock, so he kept going, down the hall to his own bedroom, and went to bed.

CHAPTER TWENTY-ONE

The next morning, Lillian went to the nursery to find Bella just waking from her night's sleep, Sukey holding her in her arms while Bella used her little fists to rub her eyes.

"Oh, madam," Sukey said, her eyes widening at seeing her. "There was no call for you to come to us. I thought I was to care for the little one until this afternoon, at least."

Lillian felt herself blushing. "I can take her now."

"Yes, ma'am. Shall I be around to put her down for her nap?"

"Yes, that will be fine."

Bella wrapped her arms around Lillian's neck and laid her cheek against hers as they went back to Lillian's room, where she dressed Bella and listened to her chatter on. But in spite of Bella's cheerful voice, Lillian's heart seemed to be made of stone, weighing her down and creating an ache in her chest.

She'd left Bella to the servant's care, letting her sleep with her in the nursery, because it was her wedding night, but there had been no need. Lillian was fairly certain she had heard Nash come home the night before, pause in front of her door, and then go to his own bedroom.

Was this how their marriage would be? Pretending in front of his family and everyone else that they were married and happy, when he was not even interested in being married in all senses of the word? The worst part of it was that it brought back a flood of miserable memories, all those times when her first husband ignored her, slept apart from her, and didn't care to be in her presence.

How long would it be before everyone suspected the truth—that she and Nash were not truly married?

But she was getting the cart before the horse, as her grandfather used to say. Of course he had not wanted to come and wake her up last night. It had been late, she was already in bed, and he was undoubtedly quite tired. Things were still a bit awkward between them, after all. But tonight he would come to her and they would be truly married.

She didn't know why tears should sting her eyes, even now, at the thought of him choosing not to come to her on their wedding night.

She simply wouldn't think about it.

"Are you hungry?" she asked Bella as they went downstairs to the breakfast room, but halted on the steps. Would Lady Barrentine and Nash's sisters be there? Wouldn't they think it strange that Lillian was getting breakfast without Nash?

"Hungry, Mamma," Bella said, patting Lillian's cheek.

Just then, she heard a door open and close upstairs and footsteps. She waited a moment and Nash appeared at the top of the stairs.

"Good morning," he said, hurrying down to meet them.

Lillian breathed a sigh of relief. Now they could go down together. But her stomach did a wild flip while she remembered all the myriad feelings of the night before.

"Good morning," she said, determined not to betray her thoughts. "I trust your trip to see the Justice of the Peace went well."

"Thank you, I suppose it did." But his expression looked clouded over, and he looked away from her. "At any rate, it was uneventful. Did you sleep well?"

"I did, thank you. Did you?"

He opened his mouth, then closed it. "No, if I am honest." He smiled ruefully.

Was he not going to mention the fact that he did not come to her room? Perhaps he thought it was too awkward, but they *were* married. She hoped he hadn't forgotten.

"Dance again," Bella said, then yawned.

"Shall we dance some more?" Nash asked Bella. "You will have to ask Mildred to play for us."

"It's a bit early for dancing," Lillian said. "Let us have breakfast, shall we?" She tickled Bella's stomach, making her giggle.

"There you all are." Lady Barrentine smiled as they entered the breakfast room. "How bright and cheerful you all look. Bella, I think you brought the sunshine with you. Look." She pointed at the window, where sunlight was streaming in.

Bella looked at the food and pointed, so they sat down to eat.

The day seemed to drag on. Nash spent a lot of time

in his study with his solicitor, who had arrived just after they finished breaking their fast.

"Business matters I must attend to," Nash said, and closed himself and the solicitor up in the library where he wrote letters, met with tenants, and such.

Though overcast and windy, the weather was good enough that Lillian and Bella went for a walk.

Bella seemed especially energetic, chasing butterflies, jumping and skipping and saying, "Mamma! Look at me! I'm dancing with my husband." Then she jumped and skipped and ran around in circles.

Later, when they were walking more slowly, Bella started picking wildflowers. "Can I take these to Sukey?" she asked.

"Of course, my love. Are you enjoying your time with Sukey?"

"Yes." Bella kept picking flowers as she said, "Sukey knows a lot of games and rhymes. She taught me some." Then Bella started softly singing about the flowers she was picking, about where she was walking, and about the butterflies around her.

Thank you, God, Lillian thought to herself. Truly, it was probably best that Bella slept in the nursery and stopped sleeping with her. She did not want the child to grow up "nervous and timid," as Mrs. Courtney told her would happen if Lillian was her only caregiver and let her sleep in her bed. But when she had dismissed Bella's nurse, and especially when they moved to the cottage and were sleeping in a strange place, it had seemed like the only option. But now she was married. Things would need to change.

Her heart squeezed at the thought of not having Bella close to her. But Bella seemed perfectly happy, and that was what mattered. She would do what was best for Bella.

Lady Barrentine joined them, and Bella immediately gave her the flowers she was picking.

"Why, thank you, sweet Bella. I love them."

"I have to pick some more for Sukey now."

Lillian and Lady Barrentine joined her in picking the wildflowers, and they soon had more than enough for a large arrangement.

"We'll put these in water inside," Lady Barrentine said, "and then have our tea. Shall we?"

They all went inside, and while Bella went with Sukey to find vases for the flowers, Lady Barrentine said, "I believe Sukey will make a suitable nurse, if you think so. And in a few years we shall find her a governess. What do you think?"

"Thank you. Yes, I agree. Sukey seems very good with Bella."

Lady Barrentine smiled, and her eyes misted over. "Everything is working out so beautifully. I am so glad."

Lillian smiled but said nothing. She still couldn't get the thought out of her mind, which was sticking like a cocklebur, of the pain and disappointment of the night before, and how reminiscent it was of her first marriage.

She told herself she must not, could not think like that. After all, they'd only been married for one day. But it was impossible to evict the thought or the feeling.

~ ~ ~

Nash chafed at having to spend so much time with his solicitor.

"There are several details that must be addressed," the man told him, "concerning your marriage and the guardianship of the young child."

There were documents that had to be signed, letters to his barrister in London, not least of which was to direct him to apply to the Court of Chancery for guardianship of Bella. It was the sort of thing that Nash detested —details and matters of the law, money, possessions. But it was necessary, and he was the only one who could provide the signatures and make the decisions.

He would have made a terrible solicitor.

And that was just the sort of thought that would have angered his father, should Nash have expressed it. Why was he even thinking about what kind of solicitor he would make? He was an earl. The few times it had come to his father's attention that he wrote stories and let his sisters and mother read them, his father had seemed genuinely confused and disappointed in him.

What would his father say if he knew Nash had gotten himself and his wife shot at? In fact, Lillian had been shot in the arm, although, thanks be to God, it had only been a scratch. And all along they had thought someone was trying to kill Lillian, when in fact it was Mrs. Radcliffe's deranged fan who had been shooting at him.

"Lord Barrentine?" the solicitor said.

"Yes?"

"I was saying that this letter needs your signature."

"Yes, of course."

As he glanced over it and then signed it, he was still thinking how disgusted his father would have been with him. For once, he was inclined to agree with his father.

He started downstairs when all the decisions were made and everything was signed. When he was near the bottom, he heard his sister Mildred's strident voice, then his mother's softer one.

His mind and body balked. Having no desire to face

anyone at the moment, he turned and went out to the stables. A ride would, hopefully, help clear his mind.

CHAPTER TWENTY-TWO

At dinner, Lady Barrentine took her usual place at the upper end of the table, and Nash at the other end, with Lillian sitting at the first place beside him.

Lillian longed for her new husband to reach over and take her hand under the table. But the table was so large, it would have been difficult for him to reach her, without it being noticed that he was leaning over, so she was not surprised that he did not.

Dinner seemed to last longer than usual. Nash said very little, as Mildred spoke loudly and everyone either listened to her or replied to her. Lillian actually missed sitting by Lady Barrentine, who would often lean toward her and converse only with her.

Lillian's neck was tense and aching by the time they withdrew to the drawing room. Breaking with tradition, Nash came and sat next to Lillian on the sofa, and Mildred went to play the pianoforte.

"Forgive me," he said, speaking softly to Lillian so no one else could hear, "for my inattention today. Mother told me you and Bella picked flowers."

"We did."

He nodded at the vase at the other end of the room. "They are beautiful."

"Bella has an eye for color, I think. She told me she likes the way the pink and purple flowers look together."

He smiled, meeting her eyes. But there was a strange look in their depths, almost a sad, apologetic look. She wasn't sure what it meant.

Lillian tried not to look nervous. Why were they sitting there pretending to listen to Mildred's song? It felt silly. She both hoped—and feared—that Nash would lean over and ask her if she wanted to retire early to bed.

Following Mildred's third song, with her neck still aching, feeling tired to the bone, Lillian stood and took her leave, telling everyone, "I'm tired. Forgive me."

"Of course, darling," Lady Barrentine said. "Go on and get some rest. I'll see you in the morning."

Too afraid to look directly at Nash, she caught a glimpse of his face out of the corner of her eye. His expression looked frozen, a bit bewildered.

Well, if he didn't know what to do then she would not tell him.

She went up to her room, half expecting to see him follow her, but a glance down the staircase told her he had not.

She waited in her room, listening for his footsteps. But after nearly half an hour, she changed into her night clothes and went to bed.

She pressed her face into the pillow and sobbed. Was she all alone in this marriage, just as she'd been in the last one? What was wrong with her? Was she abhorrent? Did Nash feel nothing for her? Why did he not come to her?

God, what have I done? Have I made another terrible mistake? Please show me what to do. I cannot bear to be in another loveless marriage. I cannot.

She could not have the marriage annulled, as non-consummation was not grounds for an annulment. But how could she bear to stay here, day after day and night after night, and be ignored?

There were only two places she and Bella could go —to her cottage on the Isle of Wight, or to her brother Christopher's. But one seemed very lonely and the other tedious, as she'd have to listen to Gretchen talk on and on, quite matter-of-factly, of abusive things that had happened to her at her parents' hands, as if such things were normal and she was not even offended by them.

Still, perhaps it was preferable to staying here and being ignored. But if she left, everyone, including Lady Barrentine and Mildred and Emma, would know that something was amiss between her and Nash. And she could not bear to answer their questions. What would she tell them? That Nash had not come to her room once since they were married? She couldn't say that.

Then she heard it—footsteps in the hallway outside her door.

She sat up quickly. She wiped her face with her hands, sniffing and trying desperately to get rid of all evidence that she'd been crying.

The footsteps paused outside her door. But just as had happened the night before, the footsteps continued down the hall until there was only silence.

Her heart was as heavy as a stone as she lay back down and listened to her own heart beating in her ears. Too sad to cry, she closed her eyes and tried to think of a plausible excuse to go and visit her brother—without her new husband.

~ ~ ~

Nash woke up late the next morning. The sun was already high in the sky, and he jumped up and got dressed. Finally, he could spend the entire day with Lillian and Bella, with no duties or business to take care of.

He'd lain awake a long time the night before, wondering if he'd done the right thing.

Again, he had paused outside Lillian's door and listened. She'd said she was tired. Was she already asleep? He wanted to respect her privacy, to respect her right to decide when they should be together. And though it had taken him quite an effort, he'd forced himself to walk away from her door and go to bed.

Today, he had decided to take desperate measures. He'd spend the entire day with her—something his mother had told him he should do—and then, when Sukey took Bella to the nursery, he would simply ask her what she wanted. Did she want him to come to her room tonight? Or did she want to wait until they had gotten to know each other better?

He'd have to have a stiff drink first, but he could do it. He was sick of being indecisive about such an important thing. What kind of fellow was so uncertain and indecisive with his own wife? He was being ridiculous.

He went downstairs but he was so late, no one was in the breakfast room. He searched all around the house, then went outside and heard a courier galloping up the lane.

"Letter for the wife of Lord Barrentine."

"I am Lord Barrentine. I will see that she gets it. Go round to the kitchen and take some food and drink, whatever you need. A groom will care for your horse."

Nash turned and saw Mother hurrying toward him.

"Where is Lillian?" he asked.

"I believe she's in her room. She said she had a headache and did not come down to breakfast. Is that for her?" she asked, seeing the letter in his hand.

"Yes. I'll take it to her."

Nash hurried back into the house and took the stairs two at a time. He knocked on the door.

"Just a minute," Lillian called out.

"Lillian, it's me, Nash."

A few moments later, the door opened.

"Are you well?" he asked. "Mother said you had a headache and didn't come down for breakfast."

"Just a bit of a headache. It will pass." She stood in the doorway and did not invite him in.

"This just came for you." He handed her the letter.

She tore it open. "It's from my brother, Christopher." Her eyes scanned down the page. "He says something is wrong . . . That is, my sister-in-law needs someone to talk to." She looked up, her jaw set. "I need to go and try to help. I'll take Bella with me and I don't know how long we will be."

Why was she not asking him to go along?

"Is it serious? Is she sick?"

"I'm not sure exactly. My brother says, 'I need you to talk to Gretchen. She won't listen to me.'"

He peeked past her shoulder and saw that she was already packing a trunk with her clothes.

"When did you hear that something was wrong?"

"Only just now, from this letter you brought."

"But you are planning to stay overnight?"

"I am sure I will need to." She wasn't looking him in the eye. "My sister-in-law can be quite . . . strange and difficult."

"I see. I can come with you, if you wish it."

"I think it would be best if you didn't. It might embarrass my brother, depending on what is the matter."

"Very well. Shall I send a servant to help you pack your things?"

"No, thank you. I can manage."

"Well . . . let me know if I can help."

"Thank you." She finally looked him in the eye. Then she placed her hand on his shoulder, stood on tiptoe, and kissed his cheek. And just as quickly, she shut the door.

Why was she not being truthful? He hated thinking she was deceiving him, but what else could he think? She was obviously getting ready to leave before she even received her brother's note.

His heart was heavy as he turned away from her door. This day was certainly not going as he'd planned.

CHAPTER TWENTY-THREE

Lillian felt a stab of guilt as she shut the door. Had he seen her half-packed trunk behind her? If he hadn't, then Christopher's letter was like a miracle, sent to provide her a reason to leave. And yet, she could see the hurt in Nash's eyes when she said she was leaving. And she was fairly certain he had seen her trunk.

But what right did he have to be hurt? She'd cried herself to sleep the last two nights. *She* was the one who was hurt, by his lack of attention to her. She'd been his wife for the past two days and nights, and yet she'd hardly seen him.

It was strange for Christopher to ask her to come and help him with Gretchen. He'd never done anything like that before. He'd never indicated that Gretchen had a problem, and yet Lillian had many times seen her looking bleary-eyed, the way ladies looked when they took too much laudanum. It was the only time she wasn't talking.

She reread the letter, slower this time, as she paused in her packing.

I need you to talk to Gretchen. She won't listen to me. She sleeps most of the time, and when she's awake, she's sometimes cruel to Priscilla. I don't know what to do. I'm even wondering if you and Lord Barrentine might take Priscilla for a while, just until I'm sure Gretchen won't harm her.

I know it sounds mad, but I don't know who else to ask for help. Gretchen always seemed fonder of you than of anyone, so I was hoping she might listen to you.

How could anyone harm a small child like Priscilla? It was unthinkable.

Lillian hurried to the nursery to ask Sukey to help pack Bella's things, as they were going on a trip, and to let Lady Barrentine know that she had to go to her brother's house on an emergency errand. Then Lillian returned to her own packing, throwing things in her trunk, thinking more about poor Priscilla, Bella's sweet two-year-old cousin, than about what clothes she was taking.

When Lady Barrentine came to her room, Lillian gave her the letter and let her read it. "But please don't share its contents. I don't want to cause embarrassment to my brother."

"Of course not." Lady Barrentine gasped while reading it. "Oh my. And how old is Priscilla?"

"Two years old, one year younger than Bella, almost to the day."

"Oh my," she repeated in a breathy voice. "Of course you must go, and will Nash accompany you?"

"I think it best that he doesn't."

"Very well, my dear." Lady Barrentine's expression was sad.

"I shall write to you and will hopefully have good news."

"Yes, I will be waiting to hear. And I shall pray that all goes well."

"Thank you." Tears pricked her eyes as she thought about how kind Lady Barrentine had been to her. If only Gretchen had had such a kind and loving mother, or mother-in-law, perhaps things would be different for her.

~ ~ ~

Nash helped Lillian into the carriage, then transferred Bella to Lillian's arms and helped Sukey in after her.

The carriage lurched forward, and his heart seemed to lurch along with it.

He hadn't even been able to take proper leave of his wife, so quickly had she got herself ready and left. He even wondered if she'd purposely avoided taking leave of him in private.

This marriage was not going as he'd imagined or planned. He didn't blame Lillian. Things had been chaotic since the wedding. He'd had to deal with the debacle of the woman who shot at them, and now this.

Now that he thought it over, what brother would summon his sister two days after her wedding to come and help him with his wife? And, even stranger, he was almost certain Lillian had been packing to leave even before she got the letter from her brother. Was she unhappy with him?

He could hardly blame her if she was. He was in disgrace as an earl who wrote satirical novels and published them under a pseudonym. And now everyone surely knew of the crazed woman who tried to kill him on his wedding day, shooting into the small crowd consisting of his new wife, mother, and sisters. If the cartoonists enjoyed ridiculing him before, they would certainly come up with some humiliating drawings now.

Not only would the cartoons throw all decency out the window, but he could just imagine what the newspaper articles would say. "Satirical Earl Dodges Bullets While Marrying Mr. Courtney's Widow." How embarrassing for her to have her own name in the papers, and not favorably spoken of, but only used as a tool to make people laugh a bit harder at the foolish young earl who embarrassed his family and drove a young woman mad with his parodies of her favorite author's works.

"Son, are you well?"

Mother interrupted his thoughts, making him realize he was still standing in front of the house, staring after the carriage that had taken Lillian and Bella from him.

"I am well, Mother, just . . . thinking."

"Perhaps you should have gone with them," she said gently.

"I don't think she wanted me to go with her."

"Perhaps it is embarrassing for her. Such family problems often are."

But was it as embarrassing as what was happening to him in the newspapers? "Perhaps she is embarrassed by me."

"No, no. She is nothing of the kind, and you should speak to her about that, if that is what you're worried about."

He couldn't very well speak to her now. She had left.

That thought sounded petulant, but it was no less true.

"I will, Mother." He turned and went into the house,

wishing he could go back and relive the last two days differently.

~ ~ ~

Christopher greeted Lillian just inside the door. His eyes were quite red and bloodshot, his eyelids puffy, like someone who had been crying for a long period of time.

Lillian waited until Sukey had taken Bella upstairs to put her down for her nap, then asked, "Has something else happened?"

"She's gone. She left us, and I don't know where she's gone."

Lillian's heart ached to see the pain in her brother's face and hear it in his voice.

"Is Priscilla here?"

"She's in the nursery, and I think . . . I think Gretchen may have hurt her."

Lillian's stomach twisted, as if being wrung by a giant fist. "I will go up and see her."

Lillian practically ran up the stairs to the nursery. When she went inside, Priscilla was lying on her side, one arm stretched out beside her, while she played a finger game with her nurse with her other hand.

"Priscilla, your Aunt Lillian is here," Christopher said.

Priscilla only made a slight effort to turn her head and look at Lillian.

"Darling, are you well?" Lillian asked.

"It's her arm," the nurse said. "She cries when she moves it."

"Have you sent for the doctor?" She looked to Christopher.

"We weren't sure it was her arm until this morning."

"Send for the surgeon, immediately."

Christopher made a strangled sound, as if he was about to sob, then hurried from the room.

Lillian knelt beside Priscilla, who was lying on her low bed. "Priscilla, may I look at your arm?"

"No." Priscilla said, then started to moan and whimper.

"Very well, I won't touch it. I promise." Lillian could see the bruising, blue and purple blotches that covered most of her forearm.

Lillian stroked the child's forehead, brushing her blonde hair back from her face. "Would you like some milk to drink?" she asked her.

"Lemon juice."

"She wants lemonade," the nurse said. "I'll go fetch her some."

When Lillian was alone with Priscilla, she asked gently, "What happened to your arm, Priscilla? How did it get hurt?"

"Mamma, like this." Priscilla made a face, clenching her teeth, and she balled her unhurt hand into a fist.

"Was she angry when she did that?"

"Angry. Mamma hates me."

The breath rushed out of Lillian's chest, and her stomach sank.

"My sweet darling. All is well now. The physician will help your arm, and no one will hurt you again."

If she had to take Priscilla and never let her out of her sight . . .

Lillian felt as if someone had kicked her in the stomach. But she also felt red hot anger build up inside her head. She could not let this child be hurt again.

~ ~ ~

The surgeon had just packed his bag up and left after setting Priscilla's broken arm, wrapping it snugly between two small pieces of smooth wood. The poor child was sleeping, having been given laudanum, "just enough to make her sleep for a bit," the physician said.

Lillian pulled the blanket up to Priscilla's chin and went to find Christopher.

He was in the drawing room, pouring himself a glass of brandy. He was already so drunk he could barely stand.

"Christopher, I need you to tell me the truth. Has Gretchen been harming Priscilla? Or was this the first time?"

"I saw her shake her once, so hard that Priscilla fainted. That's the only time I knew of her harming her, but the nurse told me yesterday that Gretchen sent her out of the room, and . . . I don't know what you want me to say. You saw her arm." He downed the glass of golden-brown liquid in one long gulp.

"We cannot let Gretchen hurt her again. Gretchen needs help. She needs to change how she thinks before we can let her be around Priscilla again."

"Gretchen isn't here, if you haven't heard."

But she might return, and Lillian wanted to ensure she never hurt her daughter again. "Why don't you go to bed. When was the last time you slept?"

"I don't remember."

"Go and get some sleep. I'll watch over Priscilla."

Christopher sniffed, rubbed his hand over his mouth, then turned and shuffled out the door.

Lillian followed him out and watched him make his way slowly up the stairs, holding onto the railing with every step.

What should she tell the servants? They would all have heard by now that their mistress had harmed her child.

Lillian found the housekeeper and told her, "When Mrs. Hartman returns, I must be told right away, even if you have to wake me in the dead of night."

"Yes, Lady Barrentine."

She was almost startled by the name. She still was not used to it.

"And please send Priscilla's nurse to me. I wish to speak to her."

"Yes, ma'am."

When Priscilla's nurse came to her, Lillian gave her specific as well as general instructions on how to care for the child. She didn't know what influence Gretchen's actions and behavior had had on the nurse, but she wanted to make sure that she now understood that the child was to be treated gently and with love, with no harsh punishments.

Of course, a child must be disciplined and must not be allowed to misbehave or always have their own way, but after what had been done to Priscilla . . .

Lillian went up to her room to have a good cry. And when she was done, she would find Sukey and Bella and hug and kiss her daughter and thank God for her, and for sparing Priscilla any further harm.

CHAPTER TWENTY-FOUR

"I suppose you must go back home soon, to your husband, the earl," Christopher said two days later, as they stood talking in the garden where no one would hear them.

"I don't want to leave you." In actuality, it was Priscilla whom she didn't want to leave.

"I sent out a man that the constable recommended to look for Gretchen," he said. "He sent me word this morning that he found her in London." Christopher was staring across the garden, his eyes unfocused and dim. "She was in the company of a young man of our acquaintance, James Portman. She has left me and run away with him."

"I'm so sorry, Christopher. So very sorry. If there is anything I can do . . ."

"There is something. I want you to take Priscilla to live with you. And if Lord Barrentine doesn't object, I'd like him to be Priscilla's guardian."

"Perhaps you should think about this for some time before deciding."

He finally looked at Lillian. "I don't like thinking. I'd rather not think at all."

"Christopher, don't do anything impulsive."

"Divorcing my wife, for instance?"

"I was thinking more about you harming yourself. Please, take better care, and don't drink so much. I will be happy to take Priscilla back to Dunbridge Hall with me and Bella, and I can't imagine Lord Barrentine will have any objection to taking charge of Priscilla's care."

She wanted to remind him that he was Priscilla's father and that she would always need his love and affection. But in his fragile state, she decided that advice could wait. Besides, Priscilla's safety and care was paramount, and she was glad to have Christopher's permission to take charge of her, as she had swiftly come to the conclusion that she would do just that, with or without his leave.

He stared at nothing again. Finally, he said, "I can't stay here. I'm going to Bath for a while. I don't know when I'll be back."

"Bella and I will stay a bit longer here. The physician said Priscilla's bones need time to heal, and he did not advise any carriage rides until her arm had had a week to set and start to mend." Besides that, Priscilla was still so nervous about her arm, if anyone suggested a carriage ride, she might dissolve into tears and hysterics.

"Stay as long as you like. Send for Lord Barrentine. I am leaving in the morning." He started back toward the house before she could reply.

Her heart ached for him, but she did not know what she could do to help, other than make sure Priscilla was loved and properly cared for.

Her brother was in no condition to do so.

~ ~ ~

Lillian had been at her brother's home for four days when she received her second letter from Lady Barrentine, and her first letter from her husband.

She stared at his letter—her first one ever from Nash. First of many? Or first and only?

She waited until she was in her room before reading her letters, opening Nash's first.

> *My dearest Lillian,*
>
> *I hope this letter finds you well and that the problems at your brother's home have been resolved, or at least are improving. The house is very sad and dull without you. I'm forced to listen to Mildred without the benefit of your presence, which provided some protection. (Yes, she was much more polite when you were here, if you can believe it.) But I miss you and Bella more than I can say. I miss your smile, and I miss Bella ordering us to dance.*
>
> *I was grieved to hear from Mother that Priscilla's arm is broken. I am praying for her quick healing. I understand that you cannot travel, as Priscilla needs you, and because of her injury, she cannot travel. But if you do not think it would be untoward of me, I would like to come to visit you there, if it would not be too awkward for you or your brother.*
>
> *Please advise me as to your wishes in the matter. I await your answer, as your humble servant and*
> *Your Affectionate Husband,*
> *Nash*

Her heart skipped a few beats as she read the letter. She had not told Lady Barrentine any particulars as to what was happening with Christopher, Gretchen, or Priscilla, except to say that Priscilla had a broken arm and could not travel, and that Priscilla needed her and was benefitting greatly from Bella's presence.

She opened Lady Barrentine's letter, skimming over the initial greeting and description of the weather.

I am so thankful you are able to help your brother by taking charge of Priscilla's care. And I understand that you need to wait and only travel when her arm is better, the poor little dear. But I do hope you will be coming home as soon as possible. It goes without saying that I miss your company, as well as Bella's. The house is so much less cheerful without you both.

Nash also misses you very much. He has been bombarded with people sending him newspaper articles about what happened, most of which are inaccurate, to say it mildly. And the cartoons about him are just vile. He pretends not to be affected by them, but I am sure it bothers him more than he wants to admit. He has told me that he is writing to ask if he might visit you there. I hope you will say yes, for I'm sure it would be good for both of you. It has been such a short time since your wedding.

Thank you for your letters. It is so good to hear that you and Bella are well. Mildred and Emma are already planning another trip to visit relatives in London, so very soon it may be even more quiet here. I am praying for you daily.

Your affectionate friend,
Amelia

Lillian paced around the room, her heart still beating fast. Should she invite Nash to come for a visit?

Her heart had leapt at him asking if he could come. And yet, now, as she pondered, she remembered how she'd cried herself to sleep, how her mind had gone back to the way her first husband had treated her—ignoring her and barely speaking to her for days and even weeks at a time. Nash had made her feel that same feeling—hurt and disappointment, even ashamed, as if she was so unworthy, so unwanted, that even her husband couldn't deign to notice her or spend time with her.

But was that fair? Nash was nothing like her husband. Was he?

Tears came into her eyes. *God, I'm so confused. Give me wisdom.* Should she tell him the truth—that his not coming to her their first two nights of marriage had hurt her and ultimately made her angry? But that was an act of vulnerability she wasn't ready for.

She could ignore his request, or she could tell him not to come. She could say her brother could return at any time, and so might her sister-in-law, but that was not a very good excuse.

The truth was, she was all alone, with only the servants to talk to, and her brother's servants were strangely quiet. Servants were trained to only show themselves when needed, but the servants of this household were incredibly elusive, and they did their work swiftly and hurried out of the room, like skittish colts. She didn't want to assume anything, but she couldn't help but wonder if their behavior was caused from being yelled at and treated harshly.

She said a few silent prayers throughout the next hour, as she took a walk with the two nurses and Bella and Priscilla, who was still too nervous to walk outdoors and had to be carried.

They were driven inside by rain, and since the letters were all she could think about, Lillian went to her desk to answer Nash's first.

The more she had thought about it, the more she wanted Nash to come. She wanted to see him again, wanted to talk to him, wanted to have a loving and affectionate marriage, something completely different from her unhappy first marriage. And Nash would be forced to give his attention to Lillian, wouldn't he? After all, there was no one else here.

And yet, she suddenly had a wave of fear wash over her. What if things didn't go as she thought they would? What if he still refused to come to her room, to give his heart to her, to love her and be truly married to her? She wasn't sure she could bear the hurt and disappointment.

No, she was strong. She might as well know now rather than later, if indeed Nash didn't intend for their marriage to be a true and affectionate one.

She sat down and, after rereading his letter and noting his words about missing her and Bella more than he could say, she wrote to him saying she was happy for him to come for a visit, and as her brother and sister-in-law were away from home and weren't expected back for some time, she was personally inviting him. She also wrote, "I miss you as well. Bella has mentioned you every day since we left. And it is rather lonely here, with only the children's young nurses to talk to." It was as much truth as she was willing to admit in a letter.

She wrote a quick note to Lady Barrentine and sent them to Dunbridge Hall by courier so that they would arrive before nightfall.

That night she said her prayers and slept better than she had in many days.

CHAPTER TWENTY-FIVE

Nash arrived at Lillian's childhood home around midday. He'd read Lillian's letter the day before and immediately started packing his trunk, then left at dawn.

A month ago he had saved a lovely young widow from being attacked on the street of a small village, and he'd ended the month with getting shot at in the churchyard immediately after his wedding.

Now, it was time for him to behave like a man again —with bravery and truthfulness—even at the risk of rejection.

He was shown into the sitting room, where Lillian was sitting on the sofa. He caught her looking down and smoothing her skirt. When she lifted her head, her eyes sparkled and she smiled.

He advanced toward her, his heart thumping. When he drew near, she stood up and kissed his cheek.

How he longed to kiss her lips. He stared into her eyes for a long moment, but when she broke their gaze and looked down, he took her hand and kissed it instead.

"You are looking very well," he said, and had to

clear his throat, as he almost sounded as if he was growling. "Are you in good health?"

"I am. And you are well?"

"Yes."

They both sat, and he felt the awkwardness between them. But that was what he hoped to extinguish in coming here.

"Bella is on a walk with her nurse. I know she will be pleased to see you."

"And how is Bella?"

"She is very well."

"And Priscilla? Does she seem to be mending?"

"Yes, but she is still a bit nervous and protective of her arm, as one might expect, though a bit better every day, I think."

"I am glad to hear it."

The servant served them tea. Nash told her all the little messages Lady Barrentine and Emma had asked him to relay. Then Lillian asked, "Would you like to see if we might intercept the children on their walk? Luncheon will be ready soon, but I believe we have time for a walk."

"I would like that very much."

She retrieved her bonnet and they went out to the back garden. Bella saw them immediately and called out to them. She pulled Sukey's hand to hurry her along. Another servant was holding a little girl with a splint on her arm.

Bella ran the last ten yards to him, and he swung her up in his arms.

"You came to visit!" Bella squealed and squeezed his face between her hands.

"Of course I came, to visit you and your mother."

When the nurse came closer with Priscilla, Nash

said, "And is this your cousin Priscilla?"

"Yes. She broke her arm."

"Good day, Priscilla. How is your arm today?"

Priscilla didn't answer, only stared solemnly back at him from her nurse's arms.

"She will want to see you dance with Mamma," Bella said.

"She will? I think it is Bella who wishes to see me dance with Mamma." Nash winked at Lillian, then tickled Bella, making her squeal with laughter.

His heart was completely restored by the way Lillian and Bella had greeted him. And he would not waste one more day—or night—on insecurity, pride, or hesitation.

~ ~ ~

Lillian's heart swelled to see the way Bella had taken to Nash, and the way he held her in his arms, seeming quite content to have her there.

"Priscilla does not talk very much," Bella said softly, her lips almost touching Nash's cheek. He seemed to take it all in stride, as if little girls wrapped their arms around his neck every day and whispered to him and patted his cheeks.

"She has you to help her tell what it is she wants, I daresay."

"Yes, I am very useful to Priscilla. I am big and strong and have two arms, see?" Bella held out her arms to show him.

"Yes you do, and I imagine Priscilla's arm will be mended very soon and she will have two strong arms again as well," Nash said.

Lillian looked back toward the house and the housekeeper appeared at the door.

"I believe it is time to eat our luncheon. Please join us." Lillian looked at Nash.

It wasn't customary for men to partake of the meal that ladies called luncheon, which occurred around one o'clock, but Nash was hungry after his journey, and he would not say no to spending time with his beautiful lady and her adorable girls.

"Of course," he said.

They all went inside, and as was Lillian's usual practice, she included Bella and Priscilla, and out of necessity, their nurses as well, in their rather informal meal.

"I hope you don't mind," she said to Nash, as they sat down in the breakfast room to a meal of cold meats, cheeses, bread, and pastries.

"Why would I mind?" He smiled back at her.

Her heart did a little stutter. Indeed, when he smiled, it stopped her breath for a moment, so handsome was he, with his intense blue eyes and his warm way of looking at her. And his lips, his very nice teeth, his strong chin and jawline, all combined to make him the most handsome man in the world.

Besides that, he was the most agreeable man with whom she'd ever been acquainted. And with him seated close beside her at the breakfast table, he made her a bit dizzy.

Perhaps she just needed to eat.

Bella kept climbing into his lap, until he moved her plate over in front of him so she could sit in his lap to eat. Sukey tried a few times to extract her, but she protested, and Nash said it was all right.

"If she is bothering you—" Lillian began.

"No, she is all right where she is. Let her be."

Lillian could only shake her head in amusement.

Soon, Bella's eyes became heavy and she laid her head on the table.

Sukey lifted her. "Time for her nap."

Bella barely protested and appeared to be asleep on Sukey's shoulder before she made it out the door. Priscilla's nurse took her and followed suit.

"Now you may eat in peace." Lillian looked at Nash.

"Truly, she was not bothering me."

"You know that my way of keeping my young child with me is not the usual way. Society would frown upon it."

"I don't care very much what Society frowns upon, and I find I'm caring less and less these days." He raised his brows and gazed at her.

"Your mother told me of the inaccurate things printed about you in the newspapers. I'm sorry you have to see that."

"I suppose, to some extent, I deserve it." He looked resigned.

"Of course you don't deserve having lies told about you publicly."

"But I realize now how ill-advised it was of me to write books that ridiculed another writer's work. Ill-advised, ignorant even. I thought I knew how ridiculous those books were. And perhaps they are, to some ways of thinking. But I've since come to see that not only should I not have had the audacity to ridicule another author's work when that author has readers who love them, but events have arisen in my own life that I once thought would never happen to me, or anyone else in England."

"Sometimes truth is more unrealistic than fiction, I suppose." Lillian said.

"You suppose correctly." He looked rueful again.

"But don't be too hard on yourself. Your books were enjoyable on their own. And any author who cannot accept a bit of criticism is, perhaps, not ready to be published in the public forum."

He gave her a half smile. "Perhaps you are right."

Sitting close beside her, he looked as if he might kiss her, as his gaze focused on her mouth. Her breath hitched in her throat. But instead, he went on.

"Still, if I wish to continue to write, I will write something else, something that does not smack of ridicule."

"I understand. But I do think you're brave to publish a book at all."

"Brave? Or foolish?"

"You are very exacting when it pertains to yourself."

"My father used to tell me, 'Everyone expects more of an earl and a peer of the realm, and you must expect more of yourself.' Those words are a part of my thinking now. But even so, I see myself as only a man."

"You are a good man," Lillian said softly. "And a good man will be appreciated by those who know him."

She wasn't sure why she said that. She hadn't planned to. But the more she became acquainted with him and his way of thinking, the more convinced she was that he was the opposite of her first husband. After all, Mr. Courtney would never have spoken of himself as "only a man," even though he wasn't a peer of the realm.

"I am glad you invited me to come for a visit," he said quietly.

"And I'm very pleased you came." Soon he was staring at her lips, and she was staring at him.

He leaned down and pressed his lips to hers in a

brief kiss, as he placed his palm against her cheek. But almost before she could open her eyes, he was kissing her again, a tender, enveloping kiss that lingered, then ended too soon.

"You are very beautiful, Lady Barrentine," he murmured, his eyes still only half open.

She wanted to say that he was handsome, but she didn't trust herself to speak, and she didn't want to ruin this moment. She wanted to remember it for a long time, the way he had kissed her, touching her cheek, and the tender look on his face—their first private kiss.

A sound from the next room—a servant cleaning, perhaps—jolted them from their daze.

"Would you like to take a turn around the garden?" Lillian said. "I can show you some of my favorite places to hide when Christopher and I were children."

"I would very much like to hear some stories about your childhood. And I would be pleased to see anything you wish to show me." His voice was a bit deeper and gruffer than usual.

Lillian took his proffered arm and walked quite close to him as they made their way out to the garden.

CHAPTER TWENTY-SIX

"My brother has not had the gardeners tend Mother's flowers, but there used to be a nice flower bed here." Lillian indicated a large plot that was now planted with shrubs.

"You and Bella are very fond of flowers, I think."

"We are." She smiled at him, and he squeezed her hand where it rested on his arm.

"If you are not too tired from your journey, I'll show you some places where my brother and I used to play."

"I am not too tired."

They walked through the garden, and Lillian spoke of her adventures with her brother, of hiding from their nurse, climbing trees, and playing all manner of games.

"One day Christopher took the salt cellar from the dining room and we sat under that tree over there and ate salt." Lillian laughed. "That is, until Cook informed our nurse and she came and led Christopher back by his ear."

"Led Christopher by the ear, but not you?"

"Christopher was older and so he was the usually the only one who was punished. It was unfair, as sometimes I was just as guilty as he was. And for another reason." Lillian bit her lip. "I never speak of this. But when we were very young, our nurse was quite cruel to us, but especially to Christopher. She beat us and locked Christopher in a dark wardrobe for long periods of time, and even punished him by taking away his food."

She had to stop to take a breath, as just speaking about it made her breath catch in her throat and brought back the few—but terrible—memories she had of that time.

"I wasn't much older than Bella when my father discovered the woman's cruelty and sent her away. Our new nurse was better, but she also punished Christopher more than me, perhaps because I was a girl, or because I was younger."

"I am so sorry that happened to you." Nash was staring down at her, his brows drawn together, forming a wrinkle above his nose.

"I don't think Christopher ever recovered from those things that were done to him, and I think that is why he drinks so much."

Nash nodded.

"And Christopher—perhaps I shouldn't say these things about him. He is my brother and I love him."

"You may speak freely with me. I shall not betray your confidence."

Lillian thought about how to tell Nash the truth of what had been happening here. She glanced around just to make sure the gardeners weren't nearby.

"Honestly, Christopher can become quite angry, and so quickly. It is frightening to see, and that is why I was surprised that . . . You mustn't tell anyone what I'm about to tell you."

"Of course."

"The last time I was here for a visit, I felt a sadness, almost a darkness, in the house. I know that sounds strange, but I also had a slight feeling that perhaps Priscilla was not being treated well, though I could see nothing wrong in how her nurse cared for her. And apparently . . ." Lillian had to take a deep breath in order to go on. "Priscilla's arm was broken when I arrived. And she said her mother did it. Apparently, Priscilla's mother had hurt her, and it was not the first time she had, according to the nurse and to Christopher."

"That is grievous indeed," Nash said, quite solemnly.

"I had never been terribly fond of Gretchen, but I never suspected her of any such thing as harming her own child. But what she did reminds me of all the stories she used to tell of her father and the things he did to her. And even her mother, according to her stories, did cruel things to her. But the way she would tell the stories—as if she did not consider them especially strange or cruel—was so odd that I would sometimes interrupt her and say, 'That is terrible! I can hardly believe your father did that and no one came to your aid.' And she would simply continue on with the story as if I hadn't said anything, or tell another, similar story. It was as if she didn't realize, and perhaps didn't wish to acknowledge, that what had been done to her was terrible and should not have been done."

"And yet, her compulsion to tell you about those things must mean something."

"Yes. Perhaps she was replaying them in her mind and was voicing her thoughts, and then, she was replaying them in her actions with Priscilla. I don't know. I only know that I must protect Priscilla now."

"Of course. Of course, we must."

Nash's expression was thoughtful, and she made note of him saying "we."

"I must also tell you that when I arrived, Gretchen was not here. She had left, and Christopher discovered she was in the company of an acquaintance of theirs, a man. It seems she has abandoned her husband and child. And Christopher, who was quite distraught, left and went to Bath. But before he went, he asked me to take charge of Priscilla. And I told him I would take her back to Dunbridge Hall with me."

"I think that is a very good plan. And if he will allow me, I will be pleased to become her guardian, as well as Bella's. They can grow up as sisters."

"I am so grateful to hear you say that, for Christopher asked if you would."

"Become her guardian?"

"Yes."

"I will, of course. It would be a privilege."

"Thank you."

The look in his eye was so noble, it made her want to kiss him again. And why should she not? But a fit of shyness came over her and she had to look away.

They had stopped walking while she was speaking, and now they resumed.

"I'm very glad you are able to talk to me about all of this, and very thankful that I can help. I hope you always feel comfortable enough with me to speak about anything that is on your mind and in your heart."

Her spirit rose inside her at his tender tone and the thoughtful words.

"I thank you. You are very good. And I hope you will always feel able to speak to me about everything that concerns you."

They were silent for a few moments as they walked along.

Lillian pointed to a large tree at the back of the garden. "Christopher and I used to climb that tree. It was easy to climb because of the low branches."

"Ah, that is a good climbing tree. I spent many hours in a treehouse when I was a boy, just looking up at the sky through the leaves and daydreaming."

"Were you already thinking up stories to write?"

"I did sometimes daydream about stories that I was writing. I think I started writing stories when I was ten or eleven. I also wrote some poetry when I was a boy, but I haven't written any poems for several years now."

"Why'd you stop?"

"I suppose I liked writing stories more." He was quiet for several moments before saying, "But I'm not planning to write any more parodies or satires, not after what has happened."

"I hope you won't stop writing. I enjoyed your books."

"I may continue to write."

Lillian waited for him to go on.

"I don't know what I will write, but I don't feel proud of those two books anymore."

"I am sure the events of the past fortnight or so have been very difficult, but I do think you can be proud of writing something that makes people smile. It is only the newspaper that began saying that your books ridiculed another writer. I doubt that woman who shot at us would have had the slightest notion that your books were a direct parody of Mrs. Radcliffe's novels. After all, your work does not directly criticize hers."

"That is generous of you, but . . . I see things differently now than I did before. And I'm not publishing anymore under the name Perceval Hastings."

"I understand." They stood in silence, gazing up at the tree she used to climb.

"I wish I could be a child again, just for an hour, so I could climb this tree." Lillian looked at Nash out of the corner of her to see his reaction.

"I don't see why you can't right now."

Lillian laughed. "I am not dressed for climbing trees."

"You could put on a riding habit. Why not?" There was a challenging glint in his eye.

"Perhaps I will, before we leave."

"In the meantime, we can sit on this branch. Shall I give you a boost?"

Lillian let him lift her up by her waist and seat her on the giant branch that jutted out from the side of the tree about three feet off the ground. Then he seated himself beside her.

"Isn't this peaceful?" she said, noting the shadiness of the spot and how they were just hidden enough by leaves to be out of sight of the house.

"I used to sit here and read."

Nash never took his eyes off her, and she finally gave in to the desire to lean against him, laying her head on his chest. She could hear his heart beating, thumping rather fast, and felt her own breath quicken.

"I'm sorry our wedding day was so strange and chaotic," he said. She could feel his breath ruffling her hair.

"It was not your fault."

"I'm sorry I didn't ask you if you'd like me to come to you those first two nights."

She felt the deep notes of his voice all through her, as well as the intent of his words.

"I admit, I was hurt when you didn't."

She heard his intake of breath, as his breathing became audible.

"Forgive me." His hand was under her chin, and she lifted her face to his.

He kissed her with an intensity she hadn't known before, turning Lillian's stomach inside out as she fervently kissed him back.

How could it be that he kissed so well? Had he read a book about kissing? Perhaps he'd written it.

Her mind seemed to shut off, closing to anything other than his lips on hers.

Nash ended the kiss, still holding onto her arms as if to steady her. She was slow to open her eyes, but when she did, Nash said, "Someone is calling."

Then Lillian heard it. "Lady Barrentine!"

Her heart fluttered, this time with fear, as her thoughts went to Bella and Priscilla. Something must be wrong that a servant would be calling out for her.

Nash was off the branch and helping her down in less than a moment. He took her hand and they walked quickly into the sunlight at the back of the garden.

The housekeeper was waving her hand and hurrying toward them.

"What is it?" Lillian asked.

"A lady is here to see you, a Mrs. Courtney, ma'am."

Lillian's heart rose into her throat. She had no desire to see Mrs. Courtney. And then her mind went to Bella.

"Who is watching Bella? Is she safe?"

"Yes, ma'am. She and Priscilla are in the nursery

with Sukey and Molly."

"What could she want?" Nash murmured.

"I don't know."

As they strode toward the house, the housekeeper said, "Forgive me for disturbing your walk, but Mrs. Courtney has been waiting a quarter of an hour and has rung the bell three times to ask a dozen questions about where you are and why you have not come."

"I suppose the wait will do her good," Lillian said, then changed her tone. "I'm sorry she has been such a bother."

"She is solely to blame, not you . . . if I may say so."

Nash smiled and accompanied Lillian into the house.

"She insisted," the housekeeper said in a hushed voice, "that she must see Lady Barrentine alone, and will speak to no one else."

"Lady Barrentine is married to me now," Nash said, "and if she wishes me to accompany her, then there is naught Mrs. Courtney can say about it."

Lillian gazed up at her new husband. How good it was to have someone, finally, who cared and insisted on protecting her.

They entered the sitting room together to face Mrs. Courtney, who was on the sofa. Mrs. Courtney rudely looked Nash up and down, said nothing, then gave Lillian a sour look.

"Good day, Mrs. Courtney," Lillian said. "May I present the Earl of Bar—"

"I have met him before." Then she nodded at Nash. "Lord Barrentine."

"Mrs. Courtney. To what do we owe this unexpected visit?" Nash's voice was mild and held the disinterest one might expect as a matter of course from an earl.

"I would like to speak to my daughter-in-law alone."

"Whatever you wish to say to Lady Barrentine, you may say in front of her husband."

Lillian couldn't recall ever hearing anyone refuse Mrs. Courtney anything. She was quite impressed, while simultaneously worrying about the wrath Mrs. Courtney might unleash on them both.

"Very well," Mrs. Courtney said, defiantly staring Nash in the eye.

Lillian and Nash both sat down opposite Mrs. Courtney and waited for her to speak. Her gaze settled on Lillian as she began.

"It has come to my attention that you think that I am trying to kill you, that I hired someone to shoot you so that I could have Bella."

Lillian's insides quivered as she struggled not to look as frightened as she felt. But she resisted the urge to defend herself and waited for Mrs. Courtney to continue.

"I also know you think that man in the village attacked you because I paid him. The constable told me as much. I paid the man to frighten you. That is all. I did not give him permission to harm you. I told him to follow you and scare you, nothing more. If he were to have harmed you, it was not because I told him to. And I have not seen the man since. Furthermore, as for that poor woman who tried to shoot into your wedding party, I had nothing whatsoever to do with her or that shooting. Nothing whatsoever."

Lillian felt the blood drain from her face and could only stare at her dead husband's mother.

Though Mrs. Courtney had not looked at him once,

Nash was the first to speak. "You are admitting you paid that ruffian in the village of Gantt to frighten Lillian?"

"I paid him to frighten her, nothing more. And if anyone else asks me, I will deny it," she said hotly, raising her chin so high she had to look down her nose to see them. "I am here to tell you that I did not hire anyone to harm you, do you understand? I am not trying to kill you." She twisted her lips into an almost comical sneer. "I know that is what you believe, and if you continue to spread that lie, everyone will say you are mad."

Lillian was still so astonished she could barely think. What should she say to this woman who would come here to say such things?

"So, you did not wish to have the scandal of trying to kill us, but you will admit to trying to frighten Lillian in order to coerce her into giving you her child?"

"I admit nothing to you!" Mrs. Courtney cried, contradicting herself. "And I am withdrawing my petition for guardianship over Isabella." She stood up and glared at Lillian. "I wash my hands of you."

"Madam, if it puts your mind at ease, we know that you had nothing to do with the shooting on our wedding day. We never accused you of that."

"There was another shooting, the day before," the woman said. "I had nothing to do with that either, I tell you. Nothing."

Nash simply folded his arms in front of him and stared at her.

"I still say you killed my son, but until I can prove it, I am finished with you." She hurried from the room without taking leave of them, went quickly out the front door, and climbed into her carriage, while Lillian and Nash watched from the front door.

"She did hire that man in Gantt. I can hardly believe she would admit it to our faces." Nash's eyes were wide as he watched her leave.

"She was willing to admit it to us to prove that she had nothing to do with trying to kill us. I always knew she was bold, but this . . ." Lillian shook her head. "At least she says she won't try to take Bella away from me. As unkind as she always was, and as much as I disagreed with the way she treated Bella and Bella's cousin George, I never thought she would give up all claim to even visiting Bella."

"I suppose her hatred and pride were stronger than her love."

"Yes. How very true." She was too selfish, ultimately, to care about Bella.

Nash placed his arm around her, pulling her close to his side.

"Thank you for standing up to her. She always hated me without cause, and I was so afraid of offending her."

Nash was shaking his head. "I'm so sorry you had to endure that woman's ill treatment."

Lillian embraced him, closing her eyes. She was beginning to feel loved, and it was changing everything.

The image of a butterfly bursting from its cocoon came to mind, its wings unfurling from its cramped, uncomfortable space, as it awakened from its long sleep. Could it be that her heart would be like that butterfly, now that she was married to a good man?

Thank you, God. Please let it be so.

~ ~ ~

Nash and Lillian spent the rest of the day with Bella and Priscilla. They ate their dinner early, then, just before dinner, the nurses took them to get their baths and get ready for bed.

Nash and Lillian dined alone in the large dining room at the long table, speaking in hushed tones so as not to let their voices echo in the empty room. And all the while, Nash's heart was beating fast as he thought about their kisses from earlier in the day—and looked forward to what lay ahead.

As the meal was coming to an end, Lillian was gazing at him longer and longer. The lingering gazes made his pulse quicken.

"You are very beautiful," he said. Not a very original compliment, but the way her expression changed and became even more tender made him wonder if the room had grown warmer suddenly.

He was already leaning as close as he could, but he fastened his eyes on hers and spoke fervently.

"I know your first husband did not treat you well, but I want to love and adore you, the way you deserve, to give you everything that makes you happy."

"You must be tired from your journey," she said. Her voice sounded breathless. Her lips were parted in the most provocative way, although he didn't think she meant to look provocative. She was just so beautiful, with her perfect lips and eyes that radiated warmth and empathy.

"I am not feeling tired at the moment. But we can retire to bed if you like."

"Yes," was all she said.

They went up the stairs, their arms entwined. Before they even reached her door, Nash said what he'd been rehearsing in his head for days.

"I do not wish to make you uncomfortable, but I

would like to spend tonight with you, if you will allow me." They stopped in front of her door. "I promise not to do anything you don't want—"

"Yes. I would like that."

She opened the door and they were kissing before they could even get inside. He closed the door with his foot, holding her in his arms and kissing her mouth the way he'd been dreaming of. *Thank you, God.*

Loving her was God's design for his life, he had no doubt, and he could no longer even remember doubting it.

EPILOGUE

Two years later . . .

Lillian sat on the sofa holding her newborn baby, while Nash herded Bella and Priscilla up onto the sofa on either side of her.

"His face is so small," Bella said, reverently touching his hand, which had broken loose from the blanket he was swaddled in.

Priscilla reached out and gently stroked his head. "His hair is soft. Is he sleeping?"

"Yes." Lillian couldn't help smiling at their intent attention on their baby brother.

"We shall have to teach him everything," Bella said. "I will teach him his colors."

"I will teach him to stay away from horses' hooves," Priscilla said, no doubt remembering what happened a few weeks ago when Lillian snatched her away from Nash's horse when she got too close.

Tears pricked her eyes. It seemed she was always crying these days, as her heart swelled with gratitude for everything and everyone she saw around her. She wanted to imprint this memory on her thoughts and carry it with her always.

Nash met her gaze as he knelt beside his little family, a content smile on his perfect lips.

"I can teach him to play the pianoforte," Bella said confidently, even though she'd only just begun to learn herself.

"I will teach him to feed the birds," Priscilla said, speaking of her favorite activity, something they did every morning with Nash.

They'd attracted quite a following of birds in the garden, who seemed to know the exact moment when they would be fed and flocked to get their morning meal.

"Mamma, when will he learn to walk?" Bella said.

"We must be patient," Lillian said. "It could be a year or longer."

Bella's eyes went wide. "That is a long time."

"May I hold him?" Priscilla said.

"I want to hold him too!" Bella did not wish to be outdone by her little sister.

"You must sit there," Lillian instructed, "very close to each other. Very good."

Lillian placed the baby across both their laps, letting them wrap their arms around the snug bundle.

Bella's smile was intense, as she looked as if she would burst into laughter at any moment, while Priscilla cooed and touched his fingers.

"You both are going to be such good older sisters," Nash praised. "Well done, being so gentle."

Bella giggled. "I always wanted a baby brother."

They held the infant until Sukey came to the doorway. "Time for breakfast," she said. "Come, girls. You can see the baby later."

Nash took the baby from their arms and sat next to his wife. "Still feeling well?"

"I am well." Lillian stroked the baby's forehead. "We do need to think of a name for him."

"Anything but Nash."

"Why not Nash?"

"It's short. And I don't want him to feel as if he is being compared to his father by every person he meets."

They'd had this discussion before. "My grandfather's name was Charles. And I like Joshua."

"Joshua is not common." He seemed to think for minute. "Very well, then. If we still like Joshua by this time tomorrow, Joshua it is."

"I didn't expect you to be so agreeable," Lillian teased.

"I am very agreeable."

Lillian laughed.

"There is my favorite little grandson," Lady Barrentine swept into the room and went straight to Nash and took the baby from his arms.

"He's your only grandson," Nash reminded her.

"And therefore my favorite. Look at that grip," she said, letting him wrap his tiny fingers around her finger. "I believe he will be strong like his father and brave like his mother."

Nash looked as if he might dispute his mother's comment, but one glance at Lillian no doubt told him that she would tease him if he did.

Lillian hugged his arm, leaning into him as they sat together on the sofa. Indeed, this was what she'd always wanted, what she'd imagined for herself. She'd had to go through some terrible moments, some sad and unhappy years, to get to this point, but that only made it all the sweeter. How could she ever take her precious family for granted? How could she take Nash's love for granted? She couldn't.

Her marriage with Nash wasn't perfect, but it was good, and safe, and full of love, and she would spend the rest of her life thanking God for it.

The End

BOOK 4, COMING SOON!!!

A Stormy Season

Luke Watley lost his wife to a tragic accident. But it's beginning to seem like no accident at all. Someone murdered her, and now he must solve the mystery behind her death, or he is next.

Jane Gilchrist is maddeningly opinionated, annoyingly high-spirited, and . . . more appealing than any woman has a license to be. He seems to lose all rationality when she is near. But if he lets her get too close, she might be the next person to be killed because of his faithless first wife. He cannot let that happen, even if he has to reject the one woman who could restore his faith in womankind.

Jane is disgusted by the way women fawn all over the newly widowed Mr. Watley. She can't decide if she should hate him for being so sought after, feel sorry for him for losing his wife, or kiss him when no one is looking. Whatever she decides, it's sure to be a stormy season.

BOOKS BY THIS AUTHOR

A Perilous Plan

Book 1 in the new Regency Romantic Suspense series by New York Times bestselling author Melanie Dickerson.

Penelope Hammond finds herself a widow at the age of twenty-three, having been married five years to a man she barely knew. Her husband, David Hammond, Lord Hampstead, was a member of the House of Lords who rarely said more than a few words to her in a week's time-- and often did not come home at night.

But Lord Hampstead was from a wealthy, powerful London family with no enemies, so why was he murdered?

Penelope is a penniless widow with few friends and only her cold grandmother to lean on. When she finds herself pursued by both English officials and French spies, she doesn't know who to trust—until a handsome Member of Parliament, Henry Gilchrist, saves her from being attacked and kidnapped. Mr. Gilchrist seems so determined to help her, but can she trust him?

Henry Gilchrist seems to know more about her husband than she does--that he was unfaithful to her with a young Frenchwoman who Penelope thought was her friend, that his gambling problem had sunk him deeply in debt, and that he had stolen some very important plans that could put the entire country in danger. And now both the French and the English governments think she knows where these plans are.

Penelope had no idea that her husband stole secret plans and intended to sell to the French, but no one seems to believe her, except Henry Gilchrist. When she starts to fall in love with the handsome young Member of the House of Commons, will he be too embittered from a former lost love to accept his own growing feelings? But first they must save themselves from those who would do them harm, or there will be no future for them, either together or apart.

A Treacherous Treasure

Book 2 in the Imperiled Young Widows Regency Romance series.

Rebecca Heywood thought marriage would make her happy, but that hope was destroyed by her husband's infidelity. When he is murdered, everyone assumes it was at the hands of the angry husband of one of his paramours. Then rumors emerge of a pirate's treasure buried somewhere on their estate, and she discovers a long-lost treasure map among her late husband's grandfather's papers. Could her husband have been murdered by treasure hunters?

Thomas Westbrook hoped for a quiet life in the country after the horrors of war. But when he hears a gunshot the day after his neighbor is murdered, he finds himself coming to the aid of the young widow. Falling for the widow of his back-stabbing former friend would be a grave mistake. But he feels drawn to the kind and beautiful Rebecca, and when her life is threatened, he realizes he would do anything to save her.

Rebecca can't imagine marrying again after her husband's many betrayals. She also can't deny her feelings for Thomas Westbrook. But how can she ever trust men, attraction, or marriage again—the very things that ruined her happiness?

Rebecca and Thomas must find the treasure first, before the murderers and would-be thieves, even as their growing feelings for each other wage war against all their deepest fears.

A Spy's Devotion

Book 1 in the Regency Spies of London series.

In England's Regency era, manners and elegance reign in public life—but behind closed doors treason and deception thrive. Nicholas Langdon is no stranger to reserved civility or bloody barbarity. After suffering a battlefield injury, the wealthy, well-connected British officer returns home to heal—and to fulfill a dying soldier's last wish by delivering his coded diary.

At the home of the Wilherns, one of England's most

powerful families, Langdon attends a lavish ball where he meets their beautiful and intelligent ward, Julia Grey. Determined to maintain propriety, he keeps his distance —until the diary is stolen and all clues lead to Julia's guardian. As Langdon traces an evil plot that could be the nation's undoing, he grows ever more intrigued by the lovely young woman. And when Julia realizes that England—and the man she is falling in love with—need her help, she finds herself caught in the fray. Will the two succumb to their attraction while fighting to save their country?

A Viscount's Proposal

Book 2 in the Regency Spies of London series.

Leorah Langdon has no patience for Regency society's shallow hypocrisy and unnecessary rules, especially for women. She's determined to defy convention by marrying for grand passion instead of settling for a loveless union like her parents' or wedding a stuffy, pompous gentleman like Edward, the Viscount Withinghall. But when a chance meeting in the countryside leads to Leorah and Withinghall being discovered in his overturned carriage—alone and after dark—the ensuing gossip may force them together.

Withinghall has his reasons for clinging to propriety; his father perished in a duel with his mistress's husband, and Edward must avoid scandal himself if he wants to become prime minister. He certainly has no time for a reckless hoyden like Miss Langdon. But soon the two discover that Withinghall's coach "accident" was no such thing: the vehicle was sabotaged.

Can the culprit be brought to justice? Strong-willed Leorah and duty-driven Withinghall will have to work together if they have any hope of saving her reputation, his political career—and his life.

A Danerous Engagement

Book 3 in the Regency Spies of Londond series.

Just as merchant's daughter Felicity Mayson is spurned once again because of her meager dowry, she receives an unexpected invitation to Lady Blackstone's country home. Being introduced to the wealthy Oliver Ratley is an admitted delight, as is his rather heedless yet inviting proposal of marriage. Only when another of Lady Blackstone's handsome guests catches Felicity's attention does she realize that nothing is what it seems at Doverton Hall.

Government agent Philip McDowell is infiltrating a group of cutthroat revolutionaries led by none other than Lady Blackstone and Ratley. Their devious plot is to overthrow the monarchy, and their unwitting pawn is Felicity. Now Philip needs Felicity's help in discovering the rebels' secrets—by asking her to maintain cover as Ratley's innocent bride-to-be.

Philip is duty bound. Felicity is game. Together they're risking their lives—and gambling their hearts—to undo a traitorous conspiracy before their dangerous masquerade is exposed.

ACKNOWLEDGEMENTS

I want to thank my amazing writing accountability partners, Tina Radcliffe and Josee Telfer, for helping me stay motivated to write even when I don't feel like it! It's been an amazing year, thanks in great part to you.

I need to thank my wonderful beta readers, Natalie Nyquist, Crystal Job, Elizabeth and Rachael Waugh, Adrienne Bowling, Tatum Middleton, and Anna Bush. Thanks so much for all your help!

I'm grateful for my brainstorming helpers who happen to be my amazing family members! Farmers' children had to help in the fields in the olden days, and writers' children have to help with brainstorming. Well, they don't have to, but they do, and I'm thankful for Grace and Faith, and for my husband Aaron, for always being willing to listen to me talk out my story and to offer suggestions and ideas.

I'm so happy I get to do this writing thing full time, and that is due to my amazing readers. Thank you so much for all your support.

ABOUT THE AUTHOR

Melanie Dickerson

Melanie Dickerson is the New York Times bestselling author of Regency Romantic Suspense and Medieval fairy tale retellings. Her novels have won the Christy Award, the National Reader's Choice Award, the Golden Quill, Book Buyer's Best Award, and more.

Since she was a kid, Melanie has been writing stories involving a hero and heroine, lots of adventure, and a happily ever after ending. Now you'll find her in North Alabama watching movies with her handsome husband and her oddly calm Jack Russell terrier, writing with her accountability partners on video chat, or daydreaming about the characters and plot of her next book.

STAY IN THE LOOP!

Want to keep up with Melanie's new releases? Sign up for my newsletter here: https://landing.mailerlite.com/webforms/landing/f4e3f4 or on my website, https://melaniedickerson.com/

You can also follow me on Instagram @melaniedickerson123

Or Facebook, MelanieDickersonBooks, to stay in the know, see the book covers before anyone else, and keep up with all my latest news.

If you follow me on my BookBub or Amazon profile page, you will get an email whenever I have a new book releasing.

Thanks for keeping up with me! Feel free to message me on my social media or my website!

IMPERILED YOUNG WIDOWS

Regency Romantic Suspense by New York Times best-selling author, Melanie Dickerson.

A Perilous Plan

A Treacherous Treasure

A Deadly Secret

DISCUSSION QUESTIONS

1. Why did Lillian take her child and run away to the Isle of Wight? What would you have done in her situation?

2. What did you think of Mrs. Courtney's behavior toward her grandchildren and her son? Did Lillian have cause for concern?

3. Who was the man who followed Lillian from the Isle of Wight and accosted her in the village of Gantt? What was his motive and/or the motive of the person who hired him?

4. What was Nash, Lord Barrentine, doing in the post office in the village of Gantt? Why did he travel so far just to mail something? What was he mailing?

5. Nash said it was easier to criticize than to create. Do you agree? Why or why not?

6. Why did Nash's sister Mildred seem to dislike Lillian so much? How would you feel if your marriage prospects depended on your brother's

reputation?

7. Why did Nash decide to propose marriage to Lillian? And why did Lillian say yes?

8. When someone shot at Lillian and Nash, who did they assume was the shooter? Were you surprised when you learned who the real shooter was?

9. What was so abnormal about Gretchen's behavior and the things she said?

10. Why did Mrs. Courtney come to Dunbridge Hall to explain about hiring someone to frighten Lillian? Were you surprised she didn't even ask to see Bella, her own grandchild?

11. Why do you think Lillian never said her first husband's name?

12. What happened in Nash's past to make him nervous around women?